LOVE IS A SURPRISE!

LOVE IS A SURPRISE!

Faith Baldwin

Thorndike Press • Chivers Press
Waterville, Maine USA Bath, England

This Large Print edition is published by Thorndike Press, USA and by Chivers Press, England.

Published in 2002 in the U.S. by arrangement with Harold Ober Associates, Inc.

Published in 2002 in the U.K. by arrangement with the author.

U.S. Hardcover 0-7862-4083-0 (Candlelight Series)
U.K. Hardcover 0-7540-4872-1 (Chivers Large Print)
U.K. Softcover 0-7540-4873-X (Camden Large Print)

Originally published under the title *Letty and the Law*

This story was serialized in *Good Housekeeping Magazine* under the title of *Love Can Be A Problem*.

The text of this Large Print edition is unabridged. Other aspects of the book may vary from the original edition.

Set in 16 pt. Plantin by Minnie B. Raven.

Printed in the United States on permanent paper.

British Library Cataloguing-in-Publication Data available
ISBN 0-7862-4083-0

To Frank P. Barrett, Counsellor at Law, in friendship and gratitude and also as an apology for inflicting him with ideas, questions and manuscripts

CAST OF CHARACTERS

LETTY McDONALD — She had everything, looks, and money, and the temper of a spoiled brat! She could get what she wanted from anybody . . . except David.

DAVID ALCOTT — He was in love with the law, and he'd never had time to learn about women. He was serious and efficient . . . except with Letty.

RICHARD JAMES TALBOT — He was the most respected lawyer in New York, David's Chief, and Letty's guardian.

LULU RANDOLPH — was Talbot's secretary, and a very efficient one.

MILDRED SANTLEY — was David's secretary, not quite so efficient because she was in love.

MRS. MASTERS — was the Sheriff's wife. Her biscuits kept Letty happy in jail.

MISS SIMPSON — "Simpie" to Letty, she had taken care of the heiress since she was a baby.

VICTOR and SALLY REMSON — had no money . . . but they had Victor, Jr., and baby Janet . . . and each other.

PAT MORRISEY — got in a scrape now and then, but when they arrested him for drug-smuggling, Talbot knew Pat was innocent.

MAC — was a crackerjack man in the D.A.'s office, but he was sick, and needed a replacement.

CON — was a cat, and somebody didn't like him.

MOPEY — was only a little fish . . . but he led to bigger game.

RYAN and ADAMS — were smart cops.

CHAPTER 1

Even the ungrateful people who growl about Manhattan in the winter and grumble about it in the summer can find no fault with spring and autumn . . . at least not much. And surely none whatever with this particular bright October morning, which was a masterpiece, a flawless production. The air was so cool and invigorating that you forgot it might not be entirely clean, and the sun was generous and golden and the sky a peculiarly satisfactory blue — provided you remembered to look up. . . .

David Alcott was walking to work. He walked as if he enjoyed it, as indeed he did. The law offices for which he was headed were situated in Wall Street and he was tramping over Brooklyn Bridge, conveniently situated not too far from his modest bachelor apartment in Middagh Street. As he walked he whistled and now and then he sang, and if other hikers looked at him curiously he neither knew nor cared. The river was almost blue this morning and certainly silver. The tugs went tooting by, streetcars clanged in his ears and he was utterly content. He hadn't a care in the world because he was young — twenty-eight, to be exact — and healthy and had a job which he valued, and a profession which he loved. Also it was Monday morning.

Most of us dislike Mondays. Back to work, after the brief holiday of Saturday and Sunday. Mail on the desk. Things going wrong. You've played too hard or slept too late or seen a little too much of your family . . . or too little of your best girl. There it is, Blue Monday, staring you in the face. But this was Special Monday for David, the day on which he began work and association with Talbot . . . Richard James Talbot, one of the finest, best known, most loved and reputable lawyers in the East.

What a break, what a break, exulted David, swinging along the bridge. There were men swarming on it, at this early hour, painting the great cables. He wanted to call to them, yell at them. "Hi, guys, how's it going?" He would have waved his hat at that, if he had worn a hat. He wanted to take everyone into his confidence. He wanted to say, earnestly, "Look, did you ever hear of such a thing? . . . Here

I was plugging away as a clerk in Cather, Wilshire and Jervis, routine stuff day in, day out, preparing briefs on appeals — and, boy, if you don't know anything about that sort of paper work I'm telling you it's tough. And along comes this *Thatcher* v. *Garron* case and there's old man Talbot on the opposite side of the fence. And after awhile there's a phone call and I go to see him and . . . well, here I am, going to work with Talbot. Have you ever heard of such a thing? I'm shot with luck, that's what."

Walking along Wall Street a little later he had an eye for the girls who hurried past, on their way to offices . . . Pert little girls with new hats tilted over their eyes, pretty little girls with the courage of youth, the capacity for enjoyment, and the will to live and conquer. He loved them all that sunny October morning. He loved the world.

Talbot's office was on the twenty-second floor of a tall building and commanded a fine view. It was a good solid office, with nothing spurious or prettified about it. No fancy paneling, no startling modern furniture, no priceless rugs and invaluable etchings. It was a homely, spacious place which did not intimidate the clients. In such an office, with its curious and unusual air of

11

peace and quiet, a man, or a woman, could sit down and tell simply, without distraction, what troubled him, or her. It was more like a doctor's office than a lawyer's, yet not the office of a modish physician, rather that of the old-fashioned, if well-to-do, general practitioner.

The woman at the desk in the reception-waiting room was not young. She had gray hair and a slim figure and she had been with Talbot since he first hung up his shingle. Her name was Martha Grady and if David hadn't already liked her he would have fallen in love with her in a small boy-nice teacher fashion this morning because of her smile and her greeting . . . each welcomed him, and made him one of the family. The reception room had a welcoming look too, solid, comfortable furniture, the current magazines, papers. . . .

David made his way to his own office. *His* . . . with his name newly painted on the glass of the door. It wasn't very big, but it was what he wanted. Law books lined the walls, the desk was large, the telephone looked official, and the chair was one in which you could sprawl, at ease, provided no client sat in the chair opposite.

David went in, shut the door, and grinned idiotically at nothing. He saluted the books. He said, "Lafayette, we are here!"

Someone knocked. David said, "Come in," and endeavored to look professional. Miss Randolph came in, smiling. She was Mr. Talbot's secretary. She had been with him for twenty-two years. Her hair was still dark and her eyes behind the shell-rimmed spectacles were bright blue. She was Talbot's right hand and she wouldn't have been anything else for the world.

"Good morning," said Miss Randolph, whose inappropriate name was Lulu, "it's a grand day, isn't it?"

"One of the best," agreed David. He liked Miss Randolph, he liked everyone.

She said, "Mr. Talbot isn't in, as yet. I'll send Mildred to you, if you wish."

"Mildred?" inquired David, looking mildly startled.

Miss Randolph smiled at him. He was really a most attractive young man, very big and so youthful in appearance — he didn't look twenty-eight — and it was a long time since she had seen a young man of Manhattan with such clear direct gray eyes and with color back of the bronze of his skin . . . no city pallor here, even after two years in New York. But then she remembered, David Alcott was a country boy.

"Mildred Santley," she explained, "my niece, you remember Mr. Talbot speaking of her? She's been a typist here for three years and has been assigned to do your work."

He said, drawing a deep breath:

"I hope there's lots of it!"

"There will be." Lulu went to the door and turned. She said sincerely, "We all hope you're going to be happy here with us."

Yes, sir, as unlike a law office as possible . . . as unlike, that is, the enormous organization which boasted seven partners besides those enumerated in the firm's title, employed forty law clerks, and God knew how many underlings besides. Talbot's office in a way reminded David of that of old Judge Lynch — the local lawyer in David's upstate home town, who was also judge of probate. David had worked there when he was in high school, after school hours, copying wills and other estate matters into permanent records. Lynch's rooms had been small and crowded, noisy and filled with rank cigar smoke, but they had also been friendly. Everyone who came in knew and respected fat, genial Sam Lynch, everyone knew David. And it was in Lynch's office that David first fell irrevocably in love — with the Law.

Mildred knocked and entered. She was a small, trim girl, a little worried because of her promotion. Worried and elated . . . Talbot employed a number of typists, all experts in the sort of work they were called upon to handle, and of these Mildred had been selected to serve as David's secretary. She came in, therefore, demurely and gravely, but her anxiety and, very nearly, her gravity departed when she discerned that the big young man with the untidy shock of dark-red hair was as ill at ease as she had been.

He held out an enormous hand and her own was engulfed. She thought, Golly, he's good-looking, without however a waver in her allegiance to her special boy friend, who clerked in a broker's office not many blocks away. And David grinned at her, vastly pleased to find her a pleasant blond morsel, easy on the eyes. He said, "I'm a slave driver," warningly.

Mildred said, "That doesn't worry me, Mr. Alcott, I like work."

"You do? So do I; haven't any use for people who —" He broke off. He said, waving his hand at the desk, its polished surface bare except for a morning newspaper, the usual pen, ink, pencils, blotters, clips, and a huge ash tray. "You see, there isn't much to go on with today."

She was not, as yet, his exclusive secretary. But when he needed her, she'd be there. After a moment she departed quietly, and he watched her straight back, in its utilitarian but becoming blue serge, with appreciation. Then he sat down at his desk and opened the paper. One thing about walking to work, you didn't get to read your paper; and he had overslept this morning, so had not lingered over coffee.

He looked at the headlines and grunted. Everything getting worse all the time. But even the state of the world in general and the nation in particular couldn't disturb him this morning. He scrambled through the pages to look at the sports news. He glanced at shipping, for no good reason except that he always looked at the shipping, and was turning back to the front page again when on the second page a picture caught his attention.

"Home from England" was the head caption over the picture and beneath it the information that Miss Letty McDonald, well known in Manhattan society, had returned from a protracted visit abroad.

Miss McDonald had been snapped on

the liner which had brought her home. She showed considerable of her very lovely legs. She wore the most astonishing atrocity on top of her head. David viewed it critically. It was probably intended to be a hat. Its design had been fathered in a mad house; instead of cutting out paper dolls nowadays, he reflected, the inmates make hats. Around her neck she wore several yards of expensive fur which had once been four harmless animals. She was laughing and exhibited what looked like excellent teeth.

There was a little piece about her. Social item. David didn't read social items. He skimmed through this one with disapproval: visiting her mother the Honorable Mrs. Frederick Mott-Jordan . . . Cannes . . . London . . . the Lido. Something about "popular debutante of some years ago, debut in London, presentation at court." Something equally inane about a *pied-a-terre* on Sutton Place and a home at Rivermead, Connecticut.

"Nuts!" commented David and turned back to the front page. If there was one thing he disliked more than another it was a Society Girl or a Glamour Girl. Not that he knew any, intimately. But when he worked with Cather, Wilshire and Jervis he had been occasionally pressed into service to decorate a stag line. Mesdames Cather, Wilshire and Jervis had flocks of daughters and gave flocks of parties. It was well understood that they could ring up the office and demand presentable young men. All the young law clerks at C. W. and J.'s were naturally university graduates, spoke the King's English, and possessed black ties. A few of them even ran to white. David had rebelled against this ex officio activity. "But," argued his colleagues earnestly, "its done and it helps." "How in hell," David had demanded, "could it help?" And they cited instances. So-and-so, who had married twenty millions. This one, who had copped off the daughter of one of the more junior partners. That one, who had assisted an elderly gentleman out of a ballroom and sobered him up before taking him home to face his wife. That Samaritan act had brought fifty thousand dollars' worth of business to C. W. and J.

Well, David didn't like it — or the girls. They looked alike to him from the stag-line, even at closer range. Nails too long, too red, crazy hair-dos, silly chatter, all the current patois. Empty-headed, and worthless, he told himself again and turned the page once more to glare at the inoffensive

Miss McDonald. Even in a smudged newspaper print she was pretty. You couldn't get away from that. She was more. She was darn near beautiful and she looked straight out of the picture and laughed at you, intimately.

"Skirt's too short," muttered David, and flung the paper aside.

"What's that?" demanded Talbot, almost at his elbow and David turned with a start, and found himself flushing. He hadn't heard his chief come in.

"I knocked," apologized the older man, "but you seemed engrossed. What did you say, by the way?"

David grinned, opened the paper and pointed to Miss McDonald.

"This cheesecake. I said, 'skirt's too short.' "

"So it is," agreed Mr. Talbot, peering. He swung his glasses from a black ribbon and then put them on. He peered again. "Of course," he added, dropping the glasses, "I saw it earlier this morning. One of the things I wanted to talk to you about. What did you say, 'cheesecake'?"

David gaped. Then he shut his mouth hastily. He explained:

"That's what they call these pictures, all legs, you know, returning celebrities, movie stars, society women. I used to pal around with a fellow who did newspaper photography."

"Cheesecake," repeated Mr. Talbot reflectively. "Very expressive, means nothing. David, come in my office, will you? I haven't an appointment until eleven and I want to talk with you."

Talbot's office was big, many-windowed . . . you could look out over the river, you felt as if you were on top of the world. The chairs were comfortable and the old couch in the corner just escaped being shabby. There were law books, a great many of them, a huge globe of the world, photographs, and in a half dozen places chrysanthemums growing in pots. David recalled how his knees had shaken the first time he entered this room. He remembered Talbot's slow, measured voice, a beautiful voice, saying, "I was very much impressed by the brief you prepared in the *Thatcher* v. *Garron* case. Fine workmanship — exhaustive study went into that. As you may know, I have never had a partner nor even a junior associate, but for a long time I have been looking for someone whom I could train, someone to follow me, someone with a genuine love and respect for the law."

David would never forget that.

"Cigarette? Make yourself comfortable. There are things we must discuss. You'll find a good deal of the work dull routine . . . much as you found it at Cather's," began Talbot.

"I don't think so," said David firmly.

"Maybe not. I've always done my own digging," said the older man, with a sigh, "and liked it. Didn't depend on anyone else's brains or wit. But I'm sixty, I'm slowing up."

"You'll never slow up, sir," David told him earnestly.

Talbot smiled. If he had had a son he would have wanted a boy like this. Hardworking, ambitious, not afraid, a boy who had been over the rough spots, put himself through his university and law school, for David's father, a country doctor, had not been able to help him much. Only, thought Talbot wryly, if I'd had a son he would have had all the advantages. It's a toss-up how advantageous that would have been, judging by the sons of other men in my circumstances.

For over an hour he talked to David, about office routine, cases coming up for trial or appeal, and then he said:

"There's other work, of course, in addition. I have clients who were young when I was. I act in an advisory capacity to a number of people in different walks of life. Men with money, men with large business enterprises — and men who haven't any money and damned little business. Like the old-fashioned doctor, I take a number of charity cases, if the cause is just. And also I act as executor and trustee in a number of instances. I have never specialized, David. And I've been appointed guardian on more than one occasion for children whose parents were dead or divorced. I've only one such job now and it's one with which I need your help."

"Mine?" asked David astonished. He had a sudden vision of some nice youngster of fourteen or sixteen, orphaned, or perhaps of a family broken through divorce, a kid in some private school or other, coming to town on vacations, the sort of freckle-faced kid you could take to a ball game.

It was with a considerable jolt that he heard Talbot say quietly:

"Letty McDonald. I hadn't known she was home until this morning."

"You mean the girl in the — the girl with — ?"

"The cheesecake girl," admitted Talbot. He smiled, his lean, smooth-shaven face, long in the upper lip but tolerant and generous in the modeling of the mouth, briefly illuminated. "Exactly."

"You mean that you — that we — ?" David floundered further.

"Quite," replied Talbot, his eyes twinkling at the unusual spectacle of a young man practically in full flight at the mere thought of a pretty girl. "Her father was a friend of mine. He was fifty-eight when he married, far too old to adjust himself, and utterly engrossed in business. His wife, Rita, was thirty years his junior. Good family, no money. And Joel was remarkably well preserved. The girl was born at the end of the second year of the marriage, and when Letty was four Rita divorced McDonald in Reno. She was in a hurry, she wished to remarry. And Joel put no obstacles in her way. She married Mott-Jordan, half English, half American and twenty-six to her thirty-five."

"Disgusting," David remarked hotly.

"You're young," Talbot reminded him tolerantly. "Rita was a very pretty woman — still is for that matter, she's never looked her age — gay, vivacious, extravagant, and she had had six years of being married to a man incredibly her senior."

"Objection sustained," admitted David, grinning.

"McDonald made a handsome cash settlement but retained the custody of the child. That was their agreement. Letty was to visit her mother, whenever convenient for Rita, but there it ended. He provided the best nurse obtainable and then, less than a year later, had the first of his heart attacks. He promptly altered his will to suit the circumstances, leaving all his money in trust for Letty, a very considerable fortune, his bank and myself sharing the trusteeship, and making me guardian. The income was to be used by the trustees for Letty's support and education with the proviso that if the income proved insufficient at any time the trustees, at their discretion, could invade the principal for any further sums which might be deemed necessary. Upon attaining the age of twenty-one the income would be paid directly to Letty, quarterly, but the provision for the invasion of principal would cease. Letty is twenty-two now —" Talbot explained. "The principal does not come to her until she is thirty."

"I see," said David, and waited.

Talbot went on.

"I know very little about youngsters, David, less about girls than boys. I've acted as guardian to several boys and we've gone along very well. But Letty . . . Of course, I

24

see her rarely. She's been away a good deal of her life, camps, boarding school, visiting. Then, too, every so often she goes abroad and spends some time with her mother. She wasn't well as a child, and when she was about eight the doctors advised that she be brought up out of town; and as the trustees had the power to purchase a suitable home for her, we did so, a pleasant place on the Housatonic in Connecticut. She lived there with a governess, servants, and an amiable, reliable woman we found for her, a Miss Simpson. Miss Simpson has been with her ever since, on a salary, travels with her and, when Letty is here, runs her home for her, and acts as chaperon. The place in Connecticut has been rented during long periods when Letty was away, as, for instance, this past summer, when Letty and Miss Simpson were abroad. Letty cabled me from London that she expected to return sometime this month and wished it staffed as she expected to spend the autumn there. I suppose she'll come to town for the winter," he added, "and she'll turn up here almost any moment now." He leaned back in his chair and smiled at his young associate. "And from now on," he said firmly, "I expect *you'll* have to manage her."

"Who, me?" gasped David. "Look here, sir —"

"You'll understand her better than I do as you're much nearer her age," Talbot told him, to his horror.

And he was right, thought David when on Thursday Miss Letty McDonald blew into the office, he was darned tootin' . . . but anyone ought to be able to understand that type of girl!

Talbot had gone to Rhode Island for a holiday and David was busy in the office preparing an important brief when Miss McDonald was announced. There was a suspicion of a smile in Miss Grady's voice over the telephone. She said, "Miss McDonald to see Mr. Talbot."

"But didn't you tell her — ?" began David and then stopped. He was more curious than he would admit to himself. Besides, Talbot had told him that he must manage . . . He cleared his throat and said briskly, "In ten minutes, Miss Grady. Ask her to wait, please."

But in four minutes she had burst into his office with Mildred, protesting but ineffectual, behind her.

She cried, "If you think I'm going to sit outside and cool my heels all day — !"

Mildred stifled a terrified giggle and departed. The door closed behind her.

Letty was little, she had black hair cut short, and very curly. On the back of her head she wore something scarlet which might or might not have been a hat, her eyes were the darkest blue David had ever seen, and she was delightfully titivated. Flung around her neck were the animal skins of the photograph, and they were sable. She wore a black wool frock, a brief black jacket, and a string of pearls. And she was madder than hops.

David said, rising, "I'm sorry Miss McDonald," and smiled at her pleasantly. Letty looked at him twice, and her heart gave a little thump, and she thought, Where has Uncle Dick been hiding this all my life? and said, smiling:

"I'm sorry too. Barging in like that! But I hate to wait."

He asked, "Miss Grady told you Mr. Talbot was away?"

"He would be," said Letty. She perched on the arm of the solid chair designed to make clients comfortable. "Miss Grady said 'Mr. Alcott might see you . . .' and I said, 'He'd *better*.' So here I am!"

"So I see," David told her gravely.

"How long have you been here?" she asked.

"Since Monday."

"Like it?" she demanded. "Uncle Dick's a darling, really, even though he exasperates me beyond measure sometimes."

"Mr. Talbot has been very kind to me," said David. He added, leaning back in his chair and trying to look judicially calm and professional, "If there is anything I can do for you in his absence?"

Letty slid off the arm and into the chair. She leaned forward and fixed him with her remarkable eyes. She had, he noticed, a small dimple at the left-hand corner of her mouth. Her mouth matched her hat. She said:

"It's just money. I want an advance against my income, or don't you know about such things?"

David made a rapid mental calculation.

"Mr. Talbot has told me of your situation," he admitted. "Let me see, your quarterly payment was due the tenth of this month. This is the thirteenth."

She said, "There's a desk calendar staring me in the face. I'm perfectly aware of the date, Mr. Alcott. But I need more money . . . this quarter's already spent . . . I had to borrow from friends in London against it. You see, I bought a lot of things: these furs in Sweden and clothes in Paris. You know how it is."

"I'm afraid not," David replied, with inimical courtesy.

Letty shrugged. "What, no sisters?" she murmured. She smiled at him again and added, "And then, of course, there were customs duties . . . on the furs and the clothes and some jewelry that was made to my design. Not that I paid for everything," she said, with infuriating complacence.

"You didn't pay duty," began David, his eyebrows shooting up, "you mean, you smuggled things?"

She said, "Well, I wouldn't put it like that. You make me sound like a professional." She put her hand to her throat, looped the string of pearls, and went on. "I did add to the necklace . . . pearls are lots cheaper over there. I added these two in the middle, and slipped two off the ends . . . they'd add up to the same number, in case anyone inquired. I always carry the receipt for them when I travel. You see, my father left money to be spent in, quote, purchasing a modest string of pearls for my daughter when she attains the age of eighteen, unquote," said Letty, laughing. "The trustees took him literally. I dislike false modesty," she assured him radiantly, "even if the pearls weren't."

"Weren't what?" demanded David, dazed.

"False. Anyway, I got away with the two new ones and there were some other items, not amounting to much, tucked away here and there," she added carelessly.

David reflected. He then asked:

"I assume you knew you were breaking the law?"

"Pooh!" she said, opening her eyes wide at him. "Of course. It was fun. What the government doesn't know won't hurt 'em and, besides, they get enough out of me with taxes and all. At least they must. Whenever money's tight someone writes me that taxes have been increased. It's absurd. What's the country coming to?"

What, indeed? thought David. This was the most attractive girl he had ever seen. There may have been girls more beautiful and certainly there were girls more sensible, more worthy of respect and admiration, but this girl made him want to shake his head as though he had been struck between the eyes, this girl increased his heartbeat and his metabolism and played havoc with his pulse. Yet he disliked her heartily and disapproved of her more every passing moment. It must be a matter of bio-chemistry, he told himself, deeply concerned.

She cried, "You're annoyed with me,

you'd like to read me a lecture!"

"I'd like to put you over my knee and spank you," David declared to his own horror and in an unnaturally loud voice.

"You would, would you?" said Letty. Her eyes snapped — and so did the string of pearls. "There!" she cried. "Look what you've done!"

"What I've done? Of all the illogical —"

She was down on her hands and knees scrambling about for the round creamy glowing beads. She raised her head and her small face was as scarlet as her hat. She said, "Yes, *you*, and you might help me look."

She was, he noted despondently, graceful even in awkward positions, her small rear end defiant. He muttered something and, feeling exceptionally idiotic, got down on his hands and knees too and fumbled with his big paws for the pearls. Once they bumped heads and Letty swore mildly and David stifled a more adequate profanity. With raised heads they glared at each other for a moment, and then Letty, gently collapsing, sat back on her heels, her hands full of pearls, and shrieked with laughter. She said, almost weeping, "If you knew how funny you looked!"

Mildred took this moment to knock on

the door and to enter unbidden, with letters in her hands. She took in the situation at a glance without, perhaps, grasping it, murmured, stricken, "I beg your pardon," and fled, the letters with her.

David got to his feet, laying the pearls he had retrieved in a small ash tray on the desk. He said, "And what she'll think!" He brushed off his knees.

"She's pretty," commented Letty, still on the floor. "Your secretary, of course?"

"Why of course?" demanded David.

Letty rose, and put the pearls in the ash tray. She sat down with the ash tray in her lap and counted the pearls. She said, "They're all here," dumped them carelessly into a handkerchief, knotted it and thrust it in her enormous soft suede handbag. She then remarked, closing the handbag briskly, "And you needn't look so cross."

He said stiffly, "I wasn't aware . . ."

"You aren't aware of anything, I believe," said Letty, looking at him severely. Her hat had slid even farther back on her head. She put up a hand and pushed it forward, at a crazy angle. "Not even of the fact that you're alive. Are you or are you not going to telephone Uncle Dick, and ask him to arrange an advance?"

David shook his head.

"Sorry," he said, not at all sorry and with great satisfaction, "but it's impossible."

"Why, in heaven's name?" She began to tap a small, beautifully shod foot; a very bad sign, as Miss Simpson could have told him.

"In the first place," David answered, "I doubt if he would consider it. In the second, as I understand it, he isn't alone in his trusteeship; the bank would have something to say. In the third place, Mr. Talbot is tired and needs a rest. He was persuaded with great difficulty to take a week or so away from business and we have definite orders not to disturb him unless something of great importance arises."

"I suppose you don't think this is important," said Letty, with dangerous sweetness.

"Frankly, no," David told her.

"You make me tired!" She rose to her feet. "Of all the stuffed shirts! How old are you anyway, ninety?"

"Twenty-eight," said David, endeavoring to control his temper.

"Old enough to know better. I always thought Uncle Dick was hard-boiled about money because he was a bachelor and had never had any women around . . . that I know of," she added thoughtfully. "But young bachelors are worse. Or aren't you?" she asked suspiciously, as an afterthought.

"Aren't I what?"

"A young bachelor."

"Lord, no," he answered pleasantly, "I have a wife and six children."

"I bet she's neurotic and the children are all brats," said Letty.

Against his will the corners of his mouth began to twitch. He said, as soberly as possible:

"You should know."

"What?"

"About brats."

"Well, of all the unmitigated —" she looked at him, scowling as a child scowls. Then she laughed. "You know, I like you rather. I think you're rude and unsympathetic and impossible, but I like you. And you like me," she added smugly.

"I don't," David denied with vigor. "I don't like you at all."

"Good," said Letty. "And now that you've taken up so much of my time" — she looked at her small jeweled wrist watch — "the least you can do is take me to lunch. Uncle Dick always does."

He said, "I'm sorry, I'm afraid —"

But she was on her feet, around the desk and looking over his shoulder at the appointment pad, which was utterly blank until the hour of three o'clock. She came very close to him, her black curls bobbed almost in his face, and she was pleasantly scented with something that smelled of youth and lilacs after a spring rain. She said, "Don't tell me you have an appointment. Not until three."

He hesitated, seeking an escape.

"If you don't," she said, and stamped her foot again, "I'll scream the roof down over your head and *then* what will little Miss Blue-serge think?" She thrust her small face almost into his and positively leered at him. "You'll lose your job," she said, "making passes at clients."

David drew back in horror. Blackmail! What a girl! What to do with her. He put his hand to his breast pocket. There was, he hoped, enough in the wallet to feed an elephant, let alone five feet two and a hundred and four pounds of dynamite. He surrendered.

"All right, let's go."

CHAPTER 2

When they reached the sidewalk David's ears were scarlet, he was breathing as heavily as if he had been climbing Mount Everest. For Letty had annexed him with one fell swoop. She had dragged him, as at the tail of some triumphal chariot, through the Talbot offices, which seemed bigger than usual. She had stopped in her leisurely pace to hold converse with Miss Randolph, inquiring for her health, and the well-being of all her relatives, with the utmost solicitude while David stood by uneasily. Had he been younger he would have scuffed his shoes kicking at the nearest chair or stubbed them on the unoffending floor. As it was, he had to remember his years and dignity, so he stood still and managed a bright, inane grin when Lulu Randolph's eyes met his with a distinct inquiry and the suspicion of a twinkle. Mildred popped into his office and popped out again. She had a message for him, which she delivered to him, regarding Letty meantime with awe-struck interest. It seemed years before David found himself in the elevator.

36

The elevator was crowded, Letty stood very close to David, almost under his arm, in fact. He smelled lilacs more distinctly than ever.

By the time they reached the sidewalk it was apparent to young Mr. Alcott that he was the envy of every man who beheld his companion. He hoped that the fact would not be as obvious to her.

"Well," asked Letty, "where are we going?"

David knew a little place around the corner. It was crowded at noon, but the food was good and the service swift. He mentioned both facts and Letty wrinkled her nose. She said, "Let's go uptown."

"But —"

"Why eat surrounded by bulls and bears, to say nothing of legal lights," she inquired, "when you can escape from them?" She whistled with great efficiency for a taxi, explaining, "I'm digging my car out tomorrow, it's been in storage."

The taxi drew up and Letty hopped in, David reluctantly following. She gave an address to the driver and sat back, smiling. "Relax," she advised kindly, "you look all of a dither."

"Not at all," David assured her, "it's a great pleasure."

"If so, demonstrate," Letty ordered. "You look as if you were going to the dentist's. Or perhaps you are one of those rare souls who don't mind going to the dentist? I despise it, personally."

He might have retorted that her teeth, at least from his angle of vision, appeared perfection, so she need not worry. He did not, however, small talk and the easy compliment coming a little hard. He cleared his throat and asked her gravely about her trip.

Letty shrugged. "The usual thing," she said. "Here, there, and the next place. I was with my mother part of the time. Simpie has relatives in Wales, and went up to visit them."

"Simpie?"

"Miss Simpson. My watchdog. Of course, I don't really need her any more. After all, I'm twenty-two and thousands of girls younger than I are quite on their own. But poor old soul, she hasn't anywhere else to go."

David thought he detected a note of compassion in the casual words. Perhaps the little creature had, after all, a heart. He said approvingly:

"That's decent of you."

Letty widened her eyes. In common with

many of her generation, she dreaded being caught indulging in a moment of generosity, unselfishness, pity, sentiment — in fact, in any of the kindly emotions. It wasn't good form, so she said hastily:

"She's not too bad, really, although something of a pain in the neck. But we get along. She never puts any obstacles in my way, and it's a comfort to Uncle Dick and all the long graybeards in the bank to know that she's around. She's façade, really."

"Façade?"

"Front, camouflage, trimming."

"Where is she now?"

"At Rivermead. She went by train yesterday to see if things are ready. I thought I'd keep the house open this year . . . it's fun in winter and I haven't had a winter there for quite awhile. There's a pond for skating, and you aren't far from skiing. Of course, I won't stay there all the time, we'll take an apartment in a hotel and go up weekends."

He asked curiously, because he was really interested:

"Do you think of nothing but having a good time?"

"What else is there to think about?" she demanded.

"Oh," said David flatly. "If that's your attitude it wouldn't do any good to tell you."

"Go on, tell," she said. "I'm anxious to know what serious-minded young lawyers believe gals should think about."

He said, exasperated, "I didn't mean thinking, I meant doing."

"What should I be doing, then?" she asked relentlessly.

"A thousand things," he began heroically, and stopped.

"Name one," said Letty. "I dare you!"

"Well," said David lamely, "there's charity and . . ."

Letty giggled.

"A pound of tea in one hand and a tract in the other? Or do you think I should barge into strangers' homes to examine the lives of the underprivileged?" she asked. "Seems very impertinent to me. Or should I volunteer to wipe babies' noses or sew layettes or make myself a nuisance around a hospital? Go on, you'll have to think of something better."

He said severely, "You could occupy your mind in some way, certainly."

"I've read a book," said Letty, "believe it or not."

"Girls who have leisure," said David doggedly, "often take up — well, hobbies, classes."

"Hobbies," reflected Letty and snorted. "I don't collect things. I hate antiques. I don't like gardening. I'm not interested in learning to hook rugs, tap dance, or sing folk songs in costume. I can't sing. I don't play the piano. What else can you offer?"

He said feebly, "Languages —"

"How nice," said Letty, and surveyed him with malice. "I speak understandable English and very good French. I can make myself clear in German, Italian, and Spanish. I'm not interested in learning Chinese or Russian."

"I give up," said David.

"You'd better," she told him serenely. "And for your further enlightenment, I'm a good dancer, I play fair tennis and better golf, I can ride anything on four legs, and if I can't drive a car better than you can I'll eat my hat. I haven't got round to piloting a plane yet but perhaps I will someday. And I'm as good as two men in a boat. I can swim too. So don't start thinking of lessons. I can ski and I can skate and I bet you can't."

"I can too," said David, startled, "at least I could. I was brought up in the country."

She said, after a moment:

"Trouble with you is you're too serious. Or don't you know any girls who don't

41

work? Is it all drones and no butterflies?"

"Of course I do," said David with dignity, "lots of 'em."

"What do they do with their spare time?"

David said, "Well, they keep house or go in for a hobby or get married —"

He broke off, for she was laughing at him.

"I don't like housekeeping," said Letty. "I can't sew, I can't cook, and I wouldn't get married if — if I had the world to pick from. Perhaps that's my hobby."

"What?" asked David, bewildered.

"Not getting married, not keeping house, not having a hobby, not doing anything. Or should I join a bridge club? I can play contract," she added thoughtfully, "but I don't like it. I don't like any game in which I have a partner. I won't be told what to do and when to do it or criticized if I do it my way and it isn't my partner's idea. I like to be on my own, win, lose or draw. Beholden to no one, responsible to no one. And that's that!"

He said slowly, "I'm beginning to see."

The cab drew up, and they alighted. David paid the driver and added a normal tip. The driver did not thank him. They walked into a building on West 52nd Street.

This was Twenty-One. David had read about it but he had never been here. He watched Letty's progress. Everyone knew her. There were shrieks of greeting, on the way upstairs. It seemed hours to him before they arrived at their table. And when they did, ordering was delayed because people, male and female, kept coming over and falling on Letty's neck. Everyone kissed her. David felt stiff and awkward and in the background. He heard only his own name in the chattered introductions. At a table opposite he recognized an actress he had seen recently and eyed her with concealed reverence. The room was full of pretty women in lunatic hats, and dashing young men.

"Let's get on with it," said Letty, "and excuse the plethora of pals. If I stayed away longer most of them would have forgotten me."

She stated it as a fact and without bitterness.

"Do you mean that?" David asked, startled.

"Oh, in general. School friends, people you meet at parties, you know, the usual mob."

"I'm afraid I don't."

"You're lucky," said Letty calmly. "Half

of these people wouldn't know if I was dead or alive. I mean, when I turn up they remember. That's all. Another six months and most of them would forget my name. It doesn't matter, they all call you darling anyway. Let's order. I suppose you'll want a drink?"

"No," said David, feeling a little foolish, as if his nose had turned blue and he'd grown a long upper lip and a longer neck. "No, I don't, if you don't mind."

"Why should I?" she inquired carelessly. "I don't like it myself, at noon — or at almost any time, in fact. Of course, there are times when you have to drink or scream with boredom." She scanned the menu, ordered lavishly, and presently David voiced his wishes: a chop, a baked potato, a green salad, coffee. Letty grinned at him when the waiter had gone.

"Nice masculine meal," she commented.

"It's more than I usually eat at noon," David told her. "Crackers and milk is more my speed."

"Necessity, stomach ulcer, or reducing?" Letty inquired.

David said slowly:

"Necessity — and habit."

She said, widening her eyes again in the way she had, which sent your pulses ticking like a watch gone crazy:

"I'll speak to Uncle Dick. He ought to pay you more!"

"I beg of you, do nothing of the kind," said David hastily.

"Oh, all right," said Letty, unoffended. "McDonald knows when she's not wanted. That's Dickson over there, the writer. Hi, Dick!" She waved heartily across the room. "And that's Lina Renwick, the actress."

During luncheon she talked almost exclusively of the people nearby, regaling her companion with the latest scandal, the last word in tabletop gossip. David's head swam as if he had had the drink he refused, or several of them. He knew nothing of these people whose names fell with such familiarity from Letty's very red lips. Sitting there beside her he felt as if he were in another world, as if he had awakened on Mars.

They had finished luncheon, Letty was drinking her black coffee and smoking a gold-tipped cigarette with concentrated fury. She said presently:

"I'm sorry you didn't have a drink."

"Why?" He added, "If you mean that I'm dull company —"

"Well, you are rather," said Letty frankly. She surveyed him. "I don't know why," she mused aloud, "you're really very good-looking. But perhaps you lack the spark."

The spark was there, in his eyes. He glared at her. He said, with a repressed fury out of all proportion to the occasion:

"Would it annoy you if I told you that I personally am not concerned with your opinion of me?"

"Not at all," murmured Letty. Her smile and the dimple deepened. She said admiringly:

"You're attractive when you're angry!"

"I am not angry," denied David. He all but shouted it. The people at the next table turned around and looked pleased and interested.

"Good," said Letty. "I had hoped, however, to put you in a more mellow mood. You see —" she leaned closer to him and her eyes were enormous and pleading — "I do need that money very badly. I thought perhaps you'd relent and call up Uncle Dick."

He said firmly, "I'll do nothing of the kind. I have no right to disturb him on so trivial a matter."

"I'm glad you think it's trivial," said Letty hotly. "I'll have to use every cent of this quarter to clear my debts and run my house. And I need more."

"For what?" asked David flatly.

"Well, a new mink coat for one thing," said Letty, "if you have to be nosy."

"A new mink coat? Isn't one enough for you? I assume you have one?"

"It's a rag," said Letty despondently; "it looks as if I had slept in it — which I have, by the way — or as if it had been left out in the rain — it has, lots of times. Besides, they are styling them differently this year."

David said slowly, "I'm afraid I have no sympathy with you, Miss McDonald."

"Only to my friends," she broke in. "Call me Letty — my enemies do."

He ignored that, and went on:

"On what you paid for a mink coat which you no longer want, a family — several families — could live . . . and even eat — in what would be comparative comfort."

"Oh," said Letty, "you've been buying mink coats lately?"

"Don't be absurd," he told her shortly.

She asked, "Is it my fault that I wasn't born in a gutter? Someone has to buy mink coats, you know."

David shrugged. "You're getting beyond my depth, and" — he beckoned the waiter — "I'll have to go now, it's growing late. I'm sorry I can't do what you want. You'll have to wait until Mr. Talbot returns."

The waiter brought the check and David was under the instant impression that he had, after all, bought a mink coat. He looked at the table vaguely, as if he expected to find bits and pieces left on the plates.

"You're pretty impossible," said Letty. "So sure of yourself. Smug. Talk about the cat that swallowed the canary! You're like a canary that's managed to swallow the cat!"

"Sorry," said David stiffly.

She said, sighing:

"I hope Uncle Dick doesn't go out of town often. I'd hate to ask you to do something for me — again."

He was silent. And Letty announced, rising:

"And I won't."

"Won't what?" asked David, following her.

"Won't ask you again. I've learned my lesson. I was going to ask you if you didn't want to drive up to the country with me tomorrow. I've invited some people. It would have been a nice weekend, it will be," she said fiercely, "and I thought you might be amused. But you wouldn't be amused at anything."

His change came. He gave far too much

to the waiter in his confusion.

Letty stalked out and David followed. When they had descended the stairs he asked, "Could I call a taxi for you?"

"There's one outside," she said, "Good-by and thanks too much for lunch." Then she smiled and held out her hand. "Sorry I'm cross," she added with one of her lightning changes of mood. "Skip it, and let's be friends. It's more fun."

He took her hand, a little gingerly. He thought, poor kid, she doesn't know any better.

On the street, "Get in," she said calmly. "I'll drive you back to the office, I've nothing else to do."

So there they were again, in a taxi, sitting close together almost as if they were in the intimacy of a little room, which smelled of smoke, shabby leather and, very oddly indeed, of horses. Their driver drooped a limp cigarette from an underlip and sang happily. He was bareheaded, he wore a leather jacket, he looked like a thug with the innocent eyes of a six-year-old child, and he asked, over his shoulder:

"Want I should turn on the radio, it's Aunt Patty's Pancake Hour, and pretty good stuff, got a hot orchestra and some swell recipes."

"By all means," said Letty graciously; "we'd love to hear it."

"Drowns me out, anyhow," said the driver cheerfully. "You mustn't mind my singing. The wife's in the hospital. A boy, seven pounds. God knows how I'll send him to college," he went on, and fiddled with a dial, "but I ain't worrying about that yet."

Letty leaned forward. She asked breathlessly:

"First?"

"Sure. If it wasn't, do you think I'd be singing?"

Music blared forth, the announcer murmured sweet nothings in syrupy tones, and Aunt Patty held forth on pancakes.

"For heaven's sake!" said David helplessly.

"It doesn't hurt us," shouted Letty, "and it amuses him. I think new fathers should be amused, or don't you, Queen Victoria?"

"Now, listen to me," said David, swinging around.

"Don't hit me," said Letty. "I'll yell and the taxi driver will bop you one. He has a nice face and a new baby and his soul is full of sweetness and light, but he'd never stand seeing me bopped one by a gentleman bigger than me."

All the way downtown she sang with Aunt Patty's orchestra or listened raptly to Aunt Patty herself. David sat back and smoked furiously. This was the craziest human being he had ever encountered. He couldn't endure her. He wanted to grab her and kiss her and spank her and shake her. He hoped he'd never see her again.

When they reached the office Letty waved a hand at him. "On your way, Launcelot," she said cheerfully, "and if you change your mind about coming up to Rivermead with me, let me know. I'm leaving tomorrow morning about ten. I'm at the Waldorf."

He said, dazed:

"I thought you said you had decided not to ask me."

"I reconsidered," she said. "I think you need me in your education."

"Sorry," he told her, "I couldn't possibly. I have to work tomorrow, and besides . . ."

She said, "You know what all work and no play does? Makes Jack a rich man." She smiled again. "Well, you know where to find me if — By the way, where did you say Uncle Dick was staying?"

"At the —" He caught himself just in time. Her instant of triumph was premature. It flashed in her eyes, a dark-blue

51

gleam. He cried, "No you don't!"

"As for you," retorted Letty, "you're a wet smack. I'm glad you aren't coming. I'm sorry I asked you. Good-by, and if I don't see you until six years come next Michaelmas it will be centuries too soon."

David slammed the door and the driver gave him a wink. He said admiringly:

"Spitfire, ain't she? But they change, mister. You should have seen my Sadie before we was married."

"Drive this lady," said David with dignity, "to the nearest lunatic asylum."

On the way up in the elevator he astonished himself and everyone else by laughing heartily. He got off at his floor feeling as idiotic as his elevator companions doubtless thought him. When he reached his desk he sat down and regarded it for some time in deep thought. Mildred came in with mail and messages. The client whom he was to see at three arrived. Other things engaged his attention and it was five o'clock before he went in search of Miss Randolph.

Finding her, he asked if she could spare him a moment in his office. When they were there, with the door closed, he regarded her thoughtfully. He knew how long Lulu had been with Talbot, how trusted and trustworthy she was, and he felt he could speak his mind to her, and plainly.

"Do you know Letty McDonald well?" he asked.

"Hardly," said Lulu. "I've seen her off and on since she was an infant. Pretty, isn't she?"

"Very," said David grimly; "practically the prettiest girl I ever saw, drat her. Is she always like this?"

"Like what," demanded Lulu. "I didn't lunch with her, Mr. Alcott."

"I did," said David. His eyebrow flew up. "Wonder if it would look all right on the swindle sheet. I didn't ask her, she asked me to take her and it cost me more than my lunches for a month!"

"I'm sure," said Lulu, and laughed, "that Mr. Talbot would see it your way."

"Seriously," David went on, "I've never known such a girl."

"What did she want?" Lulu asked him practically.

"Advance on her income."

"But she's just had her quarterly."

"You're telling me! Seems she wants a new mink coat. Besides she bought a lot of stuff abroad, some of which she smuggled in. Made no bones telling me about it either."

"I wouldn't be surprised," said Lulu calmly.

"You don't condone her?"

"Of course not."

"I believe you do," said David furiously. "Women are all alike. They can be honest as the day is long every other way, wouldn't think of doing a bit of shoplifting, cheating at cards, or stealing from their friends, but when it comes to the customs!"

"That's what the chief says," admitted Miss Randolph.

"I'm glad someone agrees with me. Do you know what that girl wanted? She wanted me to call Mr. Talbot and tell him that he must arrange the advance."

"It isn't the first time," said Miss Randolph soothingly.

"She darn near got it out of me," said David gloomily, "I mean his address. I want you to tell everyone in the office who's likely to answer a telephone that she's not to know."

"All right," said Miss Randolph, "she won't know. She can wait a week anyway, she won't be arrested for debt before then. Don't worry about her, Mr. Alcott."

She left smiling, and Mildred hovering at the door plucked her sleeve. She whispered, "Did he fall for her?"

"I think so," said Miss Randolph, "somewhat as a bird falls for the glittering eye of a snake, poor kid."

She was laughing when she went back to her office next to Talbot's.

Letty was laughing too, when the next morning she stepped into her car and pulled away from the Park Avenue curb. She was laughing because it was such a fine day, because she was headed for the country in advance of her guests, and because it was fun to be twenty-two and so pretty that even doormen looked appreciative.

But she frowned, threading an expert way through traffic to the West Side, remembering that David Alcott had not called up; not that she had expected him to, but still, if he had it would have been another feather in her Scotch bonnet, which didn't need two. She wore it over one eye, with the quill in the wrong direction. She wore a checked jacket and a plain skirt and broad silver bracelets. Her pearls and her grandmother's emerald ring were in the suitcase tossed in the rumble. She had four dollars and fifty cents in her purse because she hadn't time to stop at the bank, having overslept, but her car was full of gas and oil, she had breakfasted royally, and would be home before lunch.

That's what she thought.

She didn't take Merritt Parkway. After leaving the Hudson and the Hutchinson she dawdled along back roads instead of cutting over via the Cross Country. She didn't feel like speed and parkways, she felt like narrow twisting roads, and rolling hills and the trees flaming as if torches had been set to them. She stopped in a tiny town for a soda, sat on a stool at the counter, absorbed it slowly through three straws and talked to the clerk about the state of the world. And when she got in her car again she looked at her watch and decided to step on it.

It was too bad that coming into Brookbury she was still stepping on it. She turned a corner, and there was the long wide main street and the village green and the white steeple of the church pointing the way to heaven. And also there was the parked empty car.

She was driving too fast, she cut her corner too short, she took it on two wheels and she smacked into the parked car, sideswiping it, and doing plenty of damage. She put on her brakes and alighted to survey the damage. The town constable, who wasn't far off, strolled up and surveyed her. He said:

"Well, well, that's nice, isn't it?"

"I'm sorry, officer," she began impatiently.

"You should be," said Constable Jones, "and you will. Comin' round that curve at fifty-five!"

"Fifty," said Letty, and looked stubborn.

"Fifty ain't legal in this town," said the constable. "I'll see your license, please."

Letty was stormy. She said, "It's ridiculous, I haven't time, I'm in a hurry. You can take my number. I'll stop back Monday. I've an engagement. Anyway, I'm fully insured and —"

"Listen," said Mr. Jones, "I said I wanted your license."

Letty went back to the car and snatched her handbag from the front seat. She opened it. She said, "Good Lord!" and some of the healthy color left her small face.

"Now what?" asked Constable Jones curiously.

"My license!" said Letty. "I haven't — that is —"

"Driving without a license?" said Mr. Jones smoothly. "Well, that makes it a lot better."

People had arrived, from where only

heaven knew. To Letty's knowledge, the street had been deserted a few moments ago. The accident had occurred some blocks away from the business section, where old white and yellow houses set back of wide lawns slept in the sun. Now they appeared to awaken and to swarm with people.

Small boys and big boys, all of whom, thought Letty crankily, should be in school; housewives in bungalow aprons with sweaters over them; and the owner of the damaged car, who had been calling at the house on the corner. The owner, one Miss Mehitabel Rogers, proved to be a lean lady as acidulous as a lemon drop. Miss Rogers regarded her fender and her door and announced that she'd have the law on Letty. Constable Jones intervened. He remarked simply that the law was already taking its course.

Letty said despairingly:

"But I have a license, officer, I really have."

"Leave it on the piano?" asked Mr. Jones, and was rewarded by a chuckle from the bystanders.

"No," said Letty desperately, "but you can't hold me. I mean I must go on, I'm giving a house party, I have people coming and —"

"Where's the license?" asked Constable Jones patiently.

"I've been abroad," explained Letty. "I — it lapsed, I forgot to renew it. I just returned a few days ago."

"Due in May in this state," said Mr. Jones. "I'll have to take you along, Miss —"

"But —"

He said kindly but firmly:

"Don't argue. Get in and see if you can back her out."

With much pushing, pulling and wrenching, and outside aid, Letty's car and Miss Rogers's parted company and Letty found herself driving at a stately rate of speed down the Main Street to the Town Hall with Mr. Jones stolidly beside her.

"Park here," said Mr. Jones.

Miss Rogers's car was wheezing and banging behind them. Miss Rogers wanted to be in at the death. Besides, was not her treasured car of 1928 vintage Exhibit A? She followed Letty and Jones into the Town Hall announcing that she'd show people who came careening around corners if there was one law for the rich and another for the respectable poor.

The Town Hall was a white frame building, with wide shingles. It had been standing in Brookbury for over a hundred years.

Letty was ushered into an almost empty room. There was a table in it and some straight chairs. Sunlight filtered through the windows and danced on the bare floor.

"Sit down," said the constable. He looked at Miss Rogers. "Likely to take some time, Mitty," he suggested. "Like to go on with your marketing and come back? Got to get Judge Harvest."

"He's out to his sister's," reported Mitty, "over to the home farm. Tim was taken bad in the night and the judge drove over."

"Too bad," said Mr. Jones. "And there's Dwight, I got to get him to swear out the complaint. 'Tother grand juror, Kinstead, he's in New York, visiting his boy."

Mitty said, "All right, I'll be back." She looked savagely at Letty and whispered, "Better keep an eye on her or take the key of that murdering car. She don't look to me like she'd set and wait for anyone."

Mitty's whisper had more potency than most people's shouts.

Mr. Jones took out a thumbed notebook and a stub of a pencil. He asked:

"Name please?"

"Letty McDonald."

"Miss or Mrs.?"

"Miss."

"Address?"

"I'm staying at the Waldorf Hotel in New York," Letty began, "but my home's in Rivermead. I was just on my way there. I told you I'm just home from Europe."

She turned her most dazzling smile upon him. Perhaps it would be better to dazzle a little. The constable blinked but showed no signs of softening. He said, "Pretty place, Rivermead. Seems silly to traipse around foreign countries with things so unsettled. Isn't your own good enough for you?"

He closed the notebook, and Letty asked anxiously:

"But what am I to do, officer?"

"Just wait," he advised kindly. "I've got to round up the grand juror and the judge. They'll be along presently."

Letty forgot to dazzle. She said furiously:

"But I can't."

"Sorry," said the constable; "it's the law."

"Law!" She searched violently in a well-equipped mind and dragged up a bit of dusty, unused furniture. "Couldn't I offer bail?" she inquired.

"Sure," said Mr. Jones, "if you offer enough."

She said uncertainly, "I've only four fifty — no, four-forty with me."

"Four dollars and forty cents or four hundred and forty?" he asked cautiously.

"Four dollars and forty cents," she said meekly.

Mr. Jones shook his gray head.

"Sorry. This is a criminal case," he said, "and we don't accept less than a hundred."

"Criminal!" cried Letty, aghast. "But I haven't hurt — I haven't done —"

"It's the law," he said firmly.

She drew a deep breath. "May I telephone?"

"Sure," said the constable, "all you want to. Pay station's over there."

Letty rose and went in the direction indicated. She noted that Mr. Jones strolled after her.

The telephone rang on David's desk in the office that Friday, somewhat before noon.

"This is Letty," said her voice, "Letty McDonald. I'm in Brookbury, Connecticut, at the Town Hall. Could you come at once, please, Mr. Alcott? I've been arrested!"

CHAPTER 3

David maintained a stunned silence. At the other end of the wire Letty's voice resumed, impatient and imperative:

"What happened to you, where've you gone? For heaven's sake, can't you hear me?"

He answered dully:

"Perfectly. Would you mind repeating what you just said?"

She said, with resignation:

"Don't you understand English, or is Latin your native tongue? I said I've been arrested. Listen," she added kindly, "I'll spell it for you." She did so.

"For what?" demanded David hollowly, with a complete lack of legal phraseology, to say nothing of syntax.

She said carelessly:

"I hit a car and I haven't a license. I mean, I let it lapse."

David groaned. He cried:

"How serious are the damages? Did you —" his voice shook and he lowered it — "was anyone *killed?*"

Someone knocked at his door. He didn't hear it. The door opened and Lulu Randolph stood there. He looked up, made a frantic gesture, looked away again. He sat with his ear glued to the receiver and an expression of stark horror on his pleasant face. Miss Randolph lifted an eyebrow, tightened her mental belt, and waited.

"No one was hurt," said Letty, "and I wish you'd hurry. You're my lawyer, aren't you? Or aren't you?"

"God helping me," said David, "I am. Where did you say you were? Brookbury? Very well, I'll be right along."

She ordered:

"Make it snappy."

Slowly David hung up. He swung around and perceived Miss Randolph waiting.

"Well," asked Miss Randolph, "what's wrong?"

"It's the McDonald girl," David told her, "she's been arrested."

Lulu laughed.

"No laughing matter," said David glumly, "she's hit a car, she's driving without a license."

Miss Randolph sobered. She said:

"I'm not surprised."

"Neither am I. How do I get to Brookbury? Where's Mildred?" He opened a desk drawer and searched futilely within it. "Where's a timetable?"

Lulu said practically:

"I know Brookbury. I used to visit there. The trains are few and far between. You'd better drive up."

"In my golden pumpkin?" asked David. "And where are the mice? I haven't a car. Mine fell apart last month and I haven't run to a new one as yet."

Lulu thought a moment. She said:

"I'll telephone Mr. Talbot's garage, and tell them to have the roadster ready for you. He took the big car to Rhode Island." She hesitated a moment and then added, "*You* have a license, haven't you?"

He had an idea that she was laughing at him although her mouth remained controlled; but the bright blue eyes twinkled. He snatched a wallet from his pocket and began to rake through it furiously. Women were strange. The nicest, the kindest of them were never happier than when witnessing the discomfiture of the male.

He produced the license in silence. He said, with a return to something resembling sanity, "When Mr. Talbot calls up you might tell him about this — this —" He choked and turned red.

"Interlude," suggested Miss Randolph gently.

David glared at her. He was on his feet now, snatching at a hat, a topcoat. He muttered, "Arrested!"

"And," Miss Randolph reminded him, "arresting." She added, "Watch your step, Mr. Alcott, those country judges are tough."

"Can't be tough enough to suit me," said David furiously.

He pressed a button and Mildred slithered in. He barked his orders: postpone this appointment, get that letter off, ring up So-and-so, get a messenger, send the *Hoskins* v. *Purdy* papers to his flat. He would go over them tonight. Also, he would telephone the office sometime during the afternoon. He might be able to get back, after all. He hoped so.

He flung himself out. Mildred, her blond head in a tizzy, kept saying mechanically, "Yes, sir. Certainly, Mr. Alcott, I understand . . ." and making Gregg pothooks and ovals in her notebook.

"Be calm," said her aunt in her ear, "all is not lost."

Lulu followed David out. She said quietly:

"Here's the address of the garage. I'll

call them at once."

He took the slip of paper she held out to him and turned redder than ever. He might have left the office without the slightest idea where Mr. Talbot garaged his cars. He muttered, "Thanks."

"Don't mention it," said Lulu cheerfully.

David taxied uptown, West Side, to the garage. Talbot's roadster, a long, lean maroon affair, shining and smart, was ready for him, complete with gas and oil. The attendant took a last unnecessary swipe at the gleaming windshield. He commented, "It's a swell day for a drive."

"That's what *you* think," said David. "What's the best and quickest way to get to Brookbury, Connecticut?"

The attendant told him, and produced a road map. David thanked him and drove out of the garage. The attendant shoved a dirty cap on the back of his head and whistled thoughtfully. He said, to no one in particular, "Wonder what's eatin' him?" He added, "Maybe he's heard that his wife —"

The attendant read the more lurid papers. But there was some justification for his suspicions. David did not look like a young man going for a pleasant drive in the country on a marvelous October day. Nor did he look like a young man who was going to meet his best girl. He looked like a young man going to a duel, a fire, a major catastrophe.

David drove up the causeway, along the river. He had no eyes for its sparkle. He drove over the Henry Hudson, and into Sawmill. He had no interest in the spilled ruby of woodbine, the beauty of the burning bush. He was not diverted by roadside planting.

Mr. Talbot's car was a honey. She purred along like a satisfied kitty. She was sleek and shining, well fed, and docile. At any other time David would have sung for joy, handling such a car. He did not sing and joy was not in him. Got herself arrested, did she, in order to spoil his day! He began to think that life under the Talbot banner would not be all beer and skittles. What in hell were skittles, anyway? He'd have to look that up. Perhaps working for Cather, Wilshire and Jervis had had its good points. When you were a humble clerk with C. W. and J., glamour girls didn't barge into your office, demand mink coats, spill pearls on your floor, and run up luncheon checks which would have helped materially on the last war debt or created a nest egg for the next one. Glamour girls didn't telephone you when you were busy and tell you they'd been arrested.

He spun along the Cross Country at a legal rate of speed, he swung into the Merritt Parkway, not marking its arching bridges, its rises and dippings, the dogwood trees red with berries and coppery leaves, the maples singing out in flame. He did not notice that the golden haze of the October morning had vanished and that the sky was a flame too, a steady blue flame, that the air was something to write home about. He stepped on the accelerator, absent-mindedly, and the next thing he knew he was pulling over to the side and talking to a gentleman who represented the state police.

"I know it's a fine day," said that official pleasantly, "and I know you're in a hurry to get away for the weekend; but on the other hand, is that any reason why you should exceed the speed limit?"

David was red, David was white. He said shakily:

"Good Lord, officer, I hadn't the least idea —"

"That's what they all say. Suppose you show me your license?"

David complied. He was sick with fury

and shame. Of all the damn fool . . . He said so, suddenly.

"I'm a so-and-so," he informed the officer, "I didn't mean . . . That is — well, you see," he went on, "I'm a lawyer and this morning I had a telephone call from a client. She's just been arrested, in Brookbury, and I was hurrying to —"

The officer said devoutly:

"That's a new one. Arrested?" He looked up and grinned; he was a very good-looking man. "Why?"

"Speeding," said David, stuttering slightly, "and —"

The officer laughed. He closed his notebook, in which he had not written. He said:

"Well, this time . . . on your way, buddy, and don't let it happen again."

He watched David pull out, heard his stammered thanks, saw him move, more cautiously, away. He smiled and shook his head. He didn't know whether or not to believe that one. But it was brand-new. He was tired of the old excuses. And the gentleman in the maroon roadster had looked worried, plenty. Besides, he hadn't been doing much over the limit.

At Westport David cut over and across and presently the gentle hills began to rise around him, and there were thickly wooded patches, and little rivers tinkling over polished brown stones, and clustered villages. There were old houses, and white spires, and rolling farms, and winding roads, and paddocks marked off into patterns by white hurdles. There were estates, and swimming pools, cottages, antique shops, and cabins. Now he climbed a long hill and now the road led down into a valley. Smoke rose from friendly chimneys, hung violet-blue upon the air, and evaporated into dove-gray. Stone walls fenced properties, stone walls covered with vines, stone walls half falling down, wholly delightful. A chipmunk chattered from one of them, his tiny body shaking with terror, his tail erect. A bluejay swung across the road, a flash of blue and mauve and white, shrill-voiced, indignant.

It was after two o'clock when David reached Brookbury and he was conscious of a growing emptiness. In addition to losing a day's work he had been deprived of luncheon. And as he drove into the sleepy smiling town he realized that he did not know where Letty was. Where in Brookbury did you go when you were arrested?

A constable was prowling about the bad corner, smiling negligently to himself.

71

Friday was an elegant day for arrests, almost as good as Saturday and Sunday. David, driving decorously, halted at the corner and spoke to him. He asked, pulling over, "In case I should be arrested, officer, where would I go?"

Constable Smithers gaped. Then he grinned. He inquired:

"Done somethin'?"

"No."

"Plannin' on anythin'?"

"No," admitted David, smiling in spite of himself.

"Then why worry?" asked Mr. Smithers. "We don't arrest folks in Brookbury for fun."

David sat in the parked car. Elms arched overhead. People strolled along the footpaths, separated from the roadway by wide strips of grass and trees. He said confidentially:

"It's this way, a friend of mine was arrested here, earlier today. Where will I find her?"

"Oh," said Smithers, "her! Girl with a gone-to-hell hat and plenty mad? That her?"

"Sounds like her," said David sadly.

"Driving a dark-blue roadster," amplified Smithers, "smashing into Mitty Rogers's car, right here." He indicated with a thumb. He added, "She'd be over at the Town Hall." He looked at David without envy and shook his head. "Made quite a stir, she has. Et her dinner, awhile back, with Jones beside her, watching every mouthful."

"Jones?"

"Constable."

"I see. Then," said David, with a great sigh of relief, "they've let her go on?"

Smithers shook a grizzled head. He explained patiently, "They're waitin' for the judge."

This was Alice in Wonderland. David asked to be directed to the Town Hall. Smithers complied. A moment later David parked his car in front of that venerable building and went in.

Within and without, the Town Hall slept in the sun. Gilded motes danced on the still air. The Town Hall dreamed. David, his footsteps echoing, looked about him wildly. Then he heard voices. Especially, he heard one voice, raised in impatience. "Perfectly ridiculous," it said clearly, "of all the stupid, silly —"

He shook himself as if to clear his head. He set his jaw, lowered his eyebrows, and strode in the direction of the voice.

A door stood open. David went in. There was a table, a bare floor, some straight chairs. Letty sat on one, and Mr. Jones on another. Mr. Jones's chair was tilted back. Mr. Jones was yawning. He had had a hard day.

Letty was sitting perfectly upright. The feather danced the wrong way. Her nose was freshly powdered and her cheeks were flushed. She gesticulated with her handbag. She was saying furiously, "But they're worth all kinds of money. Isn't there a jeweler in town?"

"Nope," said Mr. Jones. Then he saw David and the legs of the chair came crashing down. He asked:

"Looking for someone, bud?"

Letty turned. She leapt from the chair and ran to David. She put her hands on his arms and shook him, or tried to . . . she looked like a Pekinese worrying a mastiff. She may have been glad to see him, but David doubted it. She regarded him murderously. She cried:

"Well, you took long enough to get here!"

David freed himself. He said, "I came as fast as — as the law would allow." He swallowed twice on that, remembering the parkway and the police. "I drove, there weren't any trains."

She said absurdly, "You could have flown."

"Not without he had wings," commented Jones, an interested spectator.

Letty whirled on Mr. Jones. She said:

"This is Mr. Alcott, my lawyer." She shot David a look of concentrated hatred. "Now, perhaps you'll let me go!"

Mr. Jones arose. He said solemnly, "Name's Jones. Constable. Pleased to meet you." He extended a large horny hand and David shook it. Mr. Jones added cozily, "We're waiting for the grand juror . . . and Judge Harvest." He jerked a thumb. "Set," he invited.

"Bail," cried Letty. "He wouldn't take the pearls or Grandmother's emerald."

David looked at her. He said severely:

"Please control yourself, Miss Mc-Donald. Am I to understand that you offered bail?"

"Criminal case," explained Mr. Jones dolefully; "all she had was four dollars and forty cents. And them gimcracks."

David beamed at him. He said:

"Look, suppose you let me talk to my client . . . alone, like a good fellow."

Mr. Jones appeared doubtful. He said:

"She's a handful. I don't mean to let her

out of my sight. I don't trust her. Nor any other woman neither," he added glumly.

David said, "I'll be responsible for her, constable."

Mr. Jones viewed him with sympathy. He said:

"All right, I'll go out and close the door. I'll be right on the other side of it. Holler if you need me." He looked at the window and back again. He looked from Letty to the window. He shook his head. He said, "Well, I'll take a chance."

The door closed behind him firmly.

Letty said:

"Of all the idiotic, imbecile —"

"Wait a minute. Sit down. There. I said, sit down."

She didn't. He pushed her. She subsided, glaring. She threatened, stifled:

"If Uncle Dick were here —"

"But he isn't." David stood over her, his hands in his pockets. "Now," he said, "suppose you tell me just what occurred?"

She did so, with embellishments. She ended, "And he wouldn't take the jewelry. Said there was plenty of that at Woolworth's! Oaf! And all this time this silly judge is off somewhere and they can't get the other man, whoever he is, and I can sit here and starve."

David said unkindly:

"A gentleman named Smithers whom I met awhile back told me you had et!"

The furious little face relaxed. Letty began to laugh. She said, giggling:

"Across the street at Brookbury Tavern. With Jones in attendance. It was marvelous. I bought him his dinner too."

David refused to smile. He said:

"This is fairly serious, you know."

"I forgot about the license," she cried. "I thought the office would attend to it."

"If you forgot about it," argued David reasonably, "you didn't think anything of the kind."

"Oh, don't be so darned logical. They always attended to everything . . . the license plates, for instance."

"Well," said David, "there's no use crying over spilt licenses." He went to the door, opened it, and beckoned Mr. Jones, who came with alacrity. He said, "Okay, constable, I'll be right back."

"Where are you going?" Letty wailed.

"To get you a lawyer," David answered, over his shoulder.

Letty stamped her foot.

"I thought *you* were one. My error, I suppose."

"I am not admitted to practice in the

state of Connecticut," David told her gently. " 'Bye, I'll be right back."

Letty sat down on the straight chair again. She was crimson. Mr. Jones, lounging by the windows, chewing what appeared to be a cud, remarked genially:

"Nice fellow."

"I hate him," said Letty fiercely, "he's a fool."

"Yep, I thought you kind of liked him," said Mr. Jones, who had had plenty of experience with the unfair sex.

"Keep quiet," said Letty viciously.

David walked across the street, and down a block or so until he came to a real estate office. He went in and the gravelike calm of the small room was galvanized into life. A pretty girl smiled at him and touched her hair, two men appeared, a young man and an old one. David raised a hand and forestalled the practically inevitable. He said clearly:

"I'm not in the market for an abandoned farm, a salt box, a mansion, or an estate. I don't even want to remodel a barn or rent an office. I want a lawyer."

The older man smiled amiably. He said, "Fine, I was afraid you'd interfere with my after-dinner nap. Good lawyer right upstairs. Happens to be my son. Name's Kinney."

David went up the stairs and into an office occupied by a lean young man who was engaged in smoking a pipe and reading a paper. His feet came off the desk and he stared at David in amazement. He said, "Don't tell me, let me guess. You're a stranger in town. It's about a closing, or perhaps you've run over someone's cat. Or maybe you've just moved up here and want me to recommend a laundress, a barber, a —"

David laughed. He said:

"You speak feelingly."

"And how," said Mr. Kinney fervently.

"My name's Alcott," David told him. "I'm from New York — Richard Talbot's office —"

"R. J. Talbot?" asked Mr. Kinney, in awe.

"The same."

"I heard him argue a case once," said Kinney. "I won't forget it in a hurry. What can I do for you?"

David explained briefly.

Mr. Kinney rose. He said, more briefly, "Let's go."

CHAPTER 4

When David, with Alec Kinney, returned to the Town Hall, they found that Justice of the Peace Harvest had come back to town from the home farm and was busy answering questions about the state of his brother-in-law's health. Also, Mr. Dwight, the grand juror, had been found. Court was now in session.

Or would be, when the judge got around to it.

Kinney spoke to him privately. Judge Harvest unbent, advanced, shook hands with David. More chairs and a few interested people appeared. The door was closed. And that was that.

Mr. Dwight went into conference with Mr. Jones. David presented Kinney to Letty. Kinney's eyes widened, it was as if they had whistled. He said, in David's ear, "We don't get anything like this in Brookbury practice."

"You're lucky," said David.

The judge took his place behind the table. He was a small thin man with small sharp eyes and a small straight mouth.

The formalities complied with, Mr. Dwight as informing, or prosecuting, officer stated the complaint against one Letty McDonald: speeding, driving without a license, and inflicting damage upon private property. After this, Mr. Jones disappeared for a moment and returned with the rampant person of Miss Mehitabel Rogers.

Judge Harvest inquired whether or not the defendant was represented by counsel.

Alec Kinney, with a reassuring smile in Letty's general direction, affirmed that she was. He then asked permission to present Mr. Alcott, a practicing attorney of the New York State bar, to the court.

This all took a little time, Letty's foot tapped, and the judge frowned. He disliked impatient women. He had lived with one for thirty years. When Mrs. Judge Harvest's foot began to tap, her husband looked for fireworks and deluges, in short, ructions. He couldn't control the female Harvest foot, but he could do something about Letty's. He remarked sharply that there was entirely too much noise in the courtroom.

David rose and addressed the court. He said quietly and deferentially that he was grateful for the opportunity.

"My client, Your Honor," said David, "is young and thoughtless. She has been living out of the country for some time. She forgot that her license to drive had lapsed. She returned to the United States a few days ago and in her eagerness to be once more in her own home, in lovely River-mead, she not only omitted to remedy the matter of her license but she broke the traffic laws. She pleads guilty, Your Honor, to negligence, and to the breaking of the law — she is deeply aware of her fault, and of the seriousness of her actions, and —"

Letty spoke up clearly. She was on her feet, and her little face flew danger signals. Stop! said Letty's face, as clear as day and as red as sumac.

She said, "It's nonsense, David Alcott. You keep quiet. I've been sitting here since practically dawn and I've a right to defend myself. It wasn't my fault about the license, Mr. Alcott's office should have attended to it. And I wasn't speeding, and that woman's car had no business there, parked right at the corner!"

"Well, I never!" gasped Mehitabel.

"And," Letty went on, gaining power, "I have a right to bail only the constable wouldn't accept these." She took the shimmering pearls from the handbag, and the emerald, green as June grass, green as mountain lakes, cool, costly and aloof. "They're worth enough to bail me out of a — a murder," Letty said crossly. "Moreover, I am insured, and any damage I have done —"

Judge Harvest's jaw had dropped. He picked it up, so to speak. A gavel smote the table with a resounding crack.

"Young woman, sit down," he thundered.

"I won't," said Letty, "why should I? This is all too absurd. You'd think I'd kidnaped a baby or something. I tell you I'm *insured*. And as for the way Mr. Alcott has conducted this case —" she turned her astonishing eyes upon the gaping Kinney — "I'm sure you wouldn't have . . ."

Judge Harvest said:

"Mr. Alcott, if you cannot control your client —"

David walked over to his client. He took her by the shoulders. He said briefly, "Sit."

She sat.

David turned back to the court. Aware of Kinney's amusement, Miss Rogers's hard breathing, aware too of the keen interest of Mr. Jones and Mr. Dwight and other onlookers, and of his own great embarrassment, he said:

"I apologize for my client, Your Honor. Her conduct only bears out my point . . . that she is young, thoughtless, and impulsive. And I repeat again that she pleads guilty of the charges against her and asks for clemency, being fully aware of her —"

Letty was on her feet again. This time she shouted:

"Don't listen to him. He's fired!" She swung around and the short checked skirt swung with her. "Fired, I said," she repeated, glaring at her attorney, "and if Mr. Kinney isn't interested, I'll take my own case. No one's been injured and the insurance company —"

Judge Harvest had heard enough about the insurance company; he had heard far too much about insurance companies from the lips of traffic offenders. He was sick and tired of it. He looked at the New York attorney. He was sorry for him, he seemed a likely young man. He looked at Letty, who was still talking. If she had kept quiet the case would have been concluded briefly, with a fine and an admonition. But she hadn't kept quiet. She had talked herself into this, let her see if she could talk herself out.

He slapped the gavel down again and announced in perfectly unlegal language that he had heard enough. He said further that, in addition to her proved offenses of speeding, driving without a license, and damaging private property, Letty Mc-Donald had committed contempt of court . . .

"— with intent to disturb and interrupt said court and to insult the same, did in open court and during said trial behave in a contemptuous and disorderly manner toward said court by talking loudly and offensively, which she persisted in after being commanded to be silent —"

That would go down in the records and more too. And David, the thought of his superior suddenly heavy in his breast, stepped forward, in alarm.

"But, Your Honor," he began.

The gavel crashed again and the judge pronounced sentence.

"One hundred dollars and costs and three days in jail."

Letty began to laugh. It was no longer absurd, it was funny. It couldn't happen, it hadn't . . .

"Hush," said young Alec Kinney anxiously. Judge Harvest, his jaw even more set, was groping in the table drawer for a necessary form — a form of mittimus beginning ominously, "To the Sheriff. Greeting . . ."

"Do you mean to say," Letty demanded, as Judge Harvest, having found what he wanted, whacked his gavel again and announced that the court was no longer in session, "do you mean to say that that silly little man is actually going to put me in jail?"

"I'm afraid so," Kinney admitted seriously as the judge, having overheard, shot Letty a cold, triumphant look and, followed by the grand juror, disappeared by a back door. "I'm afraid so."

"But he can't," cried Letty. She began to stutter. "I'm a citizen," she said idiotically. "I pay taxes . . . I —"

David stood with his hands in his pockets and surveyed her. Miss Mitty, with a squeak of excitement, had departed with the rest of the audience to spread the news abroad. Mr. Jones stood quite still, his large hand hiding a mouth which may or may not have curved into an expression of merriment.

David said, "You're a resident of this state, I believe. You've committed several offenses, not the least of them being contempt of court. Had you kept quiet and permitted me to conduct this case you would have been dismissed with a fine. But you couldn't keep quiet. Oh, no, not *you*. You had to butt in. You had to babble about a fortune in jewelry and your insurance company. So what happened? So you go to jail." He added kindly, "It will be a nice, clean, quiet jail."

Letty swung around on Kinney. She said frantically:

"You can't stand there and let this — this —" Words failed her for the first time in her life. "He's fired, I tell you. You're my lawyer, now. You can get me out of this."

"I'm afraid not," said Kinney miserably. He was engaged to the pretty girl in his father's office, but Letty was so much prettier. He reminded David, "You have the right of appeal, of course."

"Not," said David smoothly, "from contempt." He grinned at Letty, he forgot that he was no longer hungry, that, instead, he had a slight but nagging headache. He said gently, "You talked yourself into this one, Miss McDonald."

John Masters, deputy sheriff, a fat and kindly man, having been summoned from an entrancing game of Chinese checkers, appeared clicking his tongue. He was grieved to find so charming a young woman in so unlikely a situation. It would, however, lend *cachet* to his jail, publicity to his town, and give his wife an opportunity to prove herself the best biscuit maker who'd ever entered her handiwork at the Danbury Fair.

Kinney said, still miserably:

"Well, if there is nothing more I can do . . ."

David gave him his card. The new card, of which he was so proud. Mr. Kinney's bill for professional services would, of course, be sent to the Talbot office.

Kinney offered his hand to Letty. He said, "If you knew how sorry . . . but the judge has had some very unpleasant experiences with out-of-town violaters of the traffic law and —"

Letty ignored the hand for a split second. Then she took it. She said, smiling:

"It wasn't your fault. If only I'd sense enough not to telephone Mr. Alcott . . . I'm sure that in *your* hands things would have had a different outcome."

Kinney stammered something and went to the door. David was talking to Masters. The door closed and Letty looked up to find the deputy sheriff gone, and herself alone with her lawyer.

She said hopefully, "Did you — ? I mean . . ."

"I didn't. You mean, did I fix it? No."

She cried, "There must be a way — money, something."

He said softly, "I don't offer bribes, Miss McDonald. Look at this thing squarely. Try to face facts, for once. You've probably broken the law all your life one way or another. This time it has caught up with you."

She said furiously, "Wait till I see Uncle Dick. You didn't even try to —"

"I did, I assure you. Had you pleaded guilty, had you kept quiet, this wouldn't have happened. If you had kept quiet even after the first warning. But you couldn't. You thought you could tell a country court that you were far superior to it, that it was ridiculous. You thought you could —"

"Oh, keep quiet," she said, "and go away. Why don't they lock me up and get it over with?"

"All in good time," said David gently. "The constable has gone to get your suitcase out of the car. The jail's right back of the Town Hall. The deputy sheriff lives next door. His wife, Mrs. Masters, acts as matron. You will be," he said gravely, "well housed and well fed. I have ascertained that there is no one in the jail at present, that is, in the section alotted to women offenders."

If she had wept, if she had implored . . . but she did neither. Tears were in her throat, tightening it. She was lonely, afraid, and very angry. Anger helped, it kept back the tears, it lessened the quality of unreality and strangeness.

She said, "I suppose they'll let me telephone."

"All you want to," said David cheerfully. "I've persuaded the authorities to give us a few moments together . . . as your counsel, you know."

"You're not my counsel." She added, after a moment, "Simpie will be frantic."

"Simpie?"

She stamped her foot again. "Miss Simpson. And I've asked people for the weekend. They'll be arriving tomorrow."

David said, "Suppose you telephone Miss Simpson and tell her you are unavoidably detained and ask her to get in touch with your guests?"

He opened the door for her and she walked out, her little shoulders square and straight. All of a sudden, for no good reason, his heart yearned over her, so small, so unyielding, so infinitely desirable and so entirely maddening. He wanted to take her in his arms, and shake her. Or perhaps he just wanted to take her in his arms. But he hadn't railroaded her into this, his conscience was clear on that score. She had railroaded herself. And it wouldn't harm her. It would teach her a lesson. It would teach her to have some respect for the Law.

The deputy sheriff stood by while Letty dropped nickels and dimes into the telephone box and explained matters to a much-bewildered Miss Simpson in Rivermead.

"Simpie? . . . I'm in Brookbury . . . I've been arrested.

"No, I can't get there for dinner, I can't get there at all, I'm going to jail . . . Jail. J-A-I-L —"

Why, she thought bitterly, must I always have to spell things for people?

"Simpie . . . Have you fainted? Are you there? Yes, *jail*. . . .

"Three days. . . .

"No, of course, I haven't killed anyone. Don't get excited, darling."

She was beginning, in a way, to see the humor of it, if only to comfort poor old Simpie who was crying and exclaiming at the other end of the wire.

"I'll like jail, I haven't had a rest for a long time. My sheriff's a darling. He looks like Porky, in the movies. . . .

"No, I haven't sent for Uncle Dick, he's away on vacation. . . .

"Yes, I have a lawyer. I have two lawyers. That's why I'm going to jail. . . .

"Never mind, skip it. Look, Simpie, you'll have to call up everyone and tell them the party's off. No, you needn't tell them why . . . not that I care. You know them all: Frank Gage, Bibi Parker, Owen Thomas. Yes, all in the book. Call them up now . . . if you can't get them, wire. They were all to arrive before lunch tomorrow. . . .

"No, I don't want you to come to see me. . . .

"Oh, all right . . . sometime tomorrow then. Hire a car at the Rivermead garage and get a good safe driver, Simpie, you know you hate driving over thirty. . . .

"No, maybe they *won't* let you in, I don't know. But you can try."

Presently she hung up, left the booth and went out to join Masters and David. Mr. Jones had come with her suitcase. He had dropped it and it had sprung open. When she reached the scene Constable Jones, red around the ears, was busy stuffing things back, delicate things, mostly silk and lace.

They were not alone, there were quite a few people hanging around Town Hall, thanks to Miss Rogers.

"That would happen," said Letty.

"It wouldn't," said David, "if you'd lock it."

She looked at him. You'd marvel how he lived after that look.

She said, in the accents one uses to a child:

"I had to unlock it to get out the jewelry. I forgot to lock it again."

The deputy sheriff had the suitcase in his large paw. He said cheerfully:

"Well, come along, Miss McDonald, we'll try to make you comfortable."

For all the world like a tavernkeeper!

She came along, with David beside her. Once she said furiously, "You needn't tag me. Go back to town and gloat."

"I'm not gloating," he said sincerely. "I'm sorry for all this. But it was your own fault, Miss McDonald."

"Thanks, too much."

"And there isn't anything I can do."

"Haven't you done enough? Yes, there is something. Would you ask Uncle Dick to stop here and see me on his way back to town? I want to ask him a favor."

He said, with a cold hand closing about his heart:

"And what would that be . . . or shouldn't I ask?"

"You shouldn't, but I'll tell you. I'm going to ask him to fire you," said Letty, "and at once. And he'll do it too."

"I doubt it," said David. But he wasn't so sure. After all, Mr. Talbot had been Letty's father's friend. He was her friend. He had been her guardian. He was still her trustee. And he, David, he'd known Talbot such a short time, he had no claim on him. And wouldn't Talbot believe he had bungled this? Hadn't he been too ready to see Letty punished? Could he perhaps have pleaded with Judge Harvest, could he have effected a suspended sentence?

He said stiffly:

"It's up to you, of course."

They had reached the corridor and a door leading to the jail. There were men in an outer room, sitting, smoking, talking. Two were playing double Canfield. One of the two sprang up, and approached Masters, drawing him aside. He was an eager youngster with unruly hair.

David said suddenly, "If I tell you I'm sorry you won't believe it — now."

"Of course not," agreed Letty.

"Hell," said the young man to the sheriff, "be a sport, give me five minutes with her, John."

"Nope," said Deputy Sheriff Masters

94

firmly. "Not three."

But the young man was at Letty's side. He was asking, "Have you a statement to make, Miss McDonald?"

"I have about fifty statements to make," said Letty, "all of them sizzling. Why? *Ugh!*"

The last was a stifled murmur of indignation. David's hand was across her mouth. He said:

"You're not talking to reporters!"

With great difficulty Letty managed to sink one small sharp tooth into his palm.

He swore, snatching it away, and Brookbury's lone reporter laughed heartily. "Gal bites lawyer," he said with relish, "if that ain't news, my name ain't Mudd."

"Of course, it ain't," said Letty crossly.

Masters chuckled.

"It's just that," he assured her. "With two d's."

He pushed Mr. Mudd gently but firmly in the chest. A door opened with a key, it shut again. Letty, David, and the deputy sheriff were on the other side of it.

This was the women's section of the Brookbury jail. Three cells. Not very large, but at least very neat.

"Here we are," said Mr. Masters genially, as if offering a suite at the Ritz.

"You'll be comfortable in here, miss, and quiet. And the wife's an A1 cook, if I do say so myself."

The last that David saw of his client was through the bars. Letty had been at bars before but never behind them. She stood there and was locked in. The deputy sheriff strolled away. He said, "I'll wait and let you out, Mr. Alcott. Mrs. Master's will be along presently. She's playing bridge or she'd have been here before."

"Well," said Letty bitterly, "I hope you're satisfied."

David looked at her through the apertures. "You'll never forgive me, will you?"

"Never. And if I don't see you for a thousand years it will be months too soon." Her eyes blazed. "It's almost worth going to jail to have you fired."

He said grimly, "If I'm fired, I'll collect one last fee" — he came closer to the bars — "and I hope Mr. Talbot will reimburse me for your fine. It's lucky I had that much with me."

"Get out, will you?" said Letty. "As I can't."

The deputy sheriff was waiting. David stepped as close as he could. She stood there, a bar in either hand, her face pressed against the steel. He bent his tall head and just managed to kiss her startled lips, the merest brush of a kiss.

"My fee," he remarked, and went toward the waiting sheriff.

CHAPTER 5

Walking with the faint suspicion of a swagger, David reached the protective presence of the deputy sheriff. He was aware of Mr. Masters's wide, revealing grin. He was aware also of a rattle behind him. The rattle was caused by Miss McDonald, shaking her bars like a hardened criminal or, perhaps, like the prettiest chimpanzee you ever saw. She was shouting, furiously, "I'll have you arrested!"

David turned and glanced her way. He inquired gravely:

"On what grounds?"

"It's an arrest, not a divorce," commented Mr. Masters with interest.

"Assault and battery," cried Letty, "or perhaps even mayhem!"

She wasn't sure what that meant, but it sounded terrible. David answered gently:

"I'd rather it were for arson."

Himself, he was in a gentle glow. Kissing, through bars, is not the most interesting form of osculation. But it had served an incendiary purpose.

Mr. Masters chuckled. He said confidentially:

"She's a pretty girl. Too bad she don't like you."

"Too bad?" gasped David, the enormity of the situation dawning upon him. "It's the best thing that ever happened to me, almost!"

The door clanged after them and was locked. The outer room was as they had left it. And Mr. Mudd was there too, buttonholing David.

"Give us a break," pleaded Mr. Mudd who, in addition to being Brookbury's lone star reporter, was also an accredited correspondent of a wire service. "Let me see your client, Mr. Alcott, and give me a statement yourself."

"I've nothing to say," answered David, and then said it in a few well-chosen words. Even a checker game stopped while the players listened with reverence.

"Whew!" said Mr. Mudd. " 'Fraid I couldn't print that. Home paper, you know, even the kiddies read it."

He grinned and dashed out of the building. Mr. Masters spoke to David kindly. "You can see her" — he jerked a massive thumb — " 'most any time you want. I wouldn't want to be too strict."

"If I never see her again," said David, in a fury, "I'll survive."

He galloped out of the Town Hall and into Brookbury's main street conscious that several not so innocent bystanders snickered as he passed. He flung himself into the maroon-colored job of his superior and set off for town. His headache was a great deal worse.

In the next village he stopped for coffee. Sitting in a small prim tearoom, waited upon by a girl who wore crinolines with determination, chewed gum and had just had a permanent, and whose brown, spectacled eyes regarded him with interest, he speculated upon his immediate dilemma. After two cups of coffee, three doughnuts, and an aspirin which he discovered in a vest pocket, slightly sticky and a little on the dusty side, he felt better. Also he knew in which direction his duty lay. He must inform Mr. Talbot at once of current events.

There was a telephone booth in the tea shop to which David repaired and fishing nickels, dimes and quarters from his pocket, he called a Rhode Island number only to be informed that Mr. Talbot was not in. Would he call later or leave his number? He would call later, he said glumly.

On the way to New York, he stopped several times to telephone and on the fourth try was successful. Talbot's unhurried voice reached him, with a heartening note of friendliness. "What's happened?" he inquired. "Mrs. Lensen have a fainting spell?"

Mrs. Lensen was a Talbot client of long standing, or, rather, sitting. She was very rich and equally neurotic. David had suffered one session with her, alone.

"No," said David, "everything's all right. Everything's fine. Except Letty Mc-Donald."

"What's she been up to?" inquired Talbot.

David gulped, gasped, and then answered as concisely as possible. There was a long silence and David cried anxiously, "Are you still there, Mr. Talbot? Can you hear me?"

"I hear you perfectly," replied Talbot without expression. "I was merely digesting this remarkable information. Arrested, you said? In jail, in Brookbury?"

David said humbly:

"I assure you I did all I could . . . but she talked herself right into it."

He was anxious, he was sweating. He said, as Talbot did not reply, "She's going to ask you to fire me. I think she'll *order* you to fire me."

"Good," said Talbot heartily, "it will give me great pleasure to deny her something."

David said feebly:

"Then you won't?"

"What's that? Speak up, boy, can't you? No, of course, I won't. Where are you, what are you doing?"

David told him:

"I'm on my way back to the office."

"It's pretty late," said Talbot mildly, "unless you wish to confer with the scrubwomen. Go home, buy yourself a good rare steak for dinner. Letty will be all right. She can commune with her soul. A little incarceration won't hurt her. I won't be at the office until Tuesday morning, but I'll drive down Monday early to see Letty. What did you say the justice's name was? . . . Harvest? How extraordinary! All right, I'll telephone him. How about reporters?"

"Mudd," said David, inarticulate with relief. What a man, what a chief, what a swell human being!

"Are you being funny?" inquired Talbot rather severely.

"No, that's his name. Mudd. He's reporter for the Brookbury weekly paper, so I don't think that —"

Mr. Talbot chuckled.

"You don't think it will go any further?" he asked. "Live and learn. But there's nothing you can do about it. The press will descend upon Brookbury in flocks, coveys, and packs tomorrow."

David cried, alarmed:

"Perhaps I shouldn't have left, Mr. Talbot. If you like I'll go back and stay."

"Nonsense," said his superior, "go home." He laughed. He laughed long and loud. He said, "All I needed to give me a really bracing holiday was this."

For the third time the operator broke in metallically, demanding more coin of the realm. David said wildly, "I haven't any . . . I mean . . ."

"Good-by," said Talbot, still laughing, "see you Tuesday."

David hung up, and in a daze of relief and hero worship returned to the Talbot car.

Driving through the blue dusk he was free to think of Letty. Until he had told Talbot, until he had some inkling of his fate, he hadn't dared think of her or of the curious sensation of cold steel against his face but something more pleasant, more exciting, if not more yielding, under his lips. Damn the girl, just thinking about her increased his metabolism!

When he reached New York, aglitter under a dark, cold sky, his headache had gone, his spirits were high. He put the car in the garage and took a taxi downtown until he found an open florist's shop, where he wired extravagant flowers to Miss Letty McDonald in care of Deputy Sheriff John Masters. The small, sad florist looked at him open-mouthed. David paid for the flowers and lengthy telegram with a flourish. He said confidentially, "She's in jail."

"You been drinking?" asked the florist, who was Greek, logical, and argued from cause to effect.

"No," said David, "but it's a good idea."

He strode out of the shop and found another telephone booth. It occurred to him that much of his recent life had been spent in telephone booths. He called Lulu Randolph at her home, after a search in the book. When she answered he told her briefly of the day's events. He ended cheerfully:

"So I'll be at the office, all day tomorrow, to clean up the letters — No, of course, I don't want Millie, it's Saturday, and she's off. And Mr. Talbot will be back Tuesday."

Lulu asked, awed:

"How'd she take it?"

"Who? Take what?"

"Miss McDonald."

"Oh . . . badly," said David happily, "very badly, indeed."

Whistling, he hung up and went off in search of a subway to Brooklyn.

He whistled to keep up his courage. A dozen times over the rare steak recommended by Mr. Talbot he thought of Letty. How did she fare, were they feeding her, was she sulking in her cell, was she in tears, would she catch cold, do herself an injury? A dozen times during the night he woke, wondered, and worried. But the thing which worried him most was the recurrent memory of the manner in which he had left her. He'd sleep and dream that it was happening all over again, only this time there were no bars. . . .

He woke from this dream pleasantly atingle and aglow. But the tingle vanished, the glow evaporated. What was Letty thinking of . . . if *she* remembered?

Letty remembered. When the clanging door had closed behind David and the deputy sheriff she sat down on the chaste white bed in her cell and rubbed her lips savagely with a scrap of monogrammed linen. Then she smiled, a small, secret, satisfied smile, rose, and opened her suitcase. She took therefrom a square black leather box and unlocked it. It contained no jewels worth a king's ransom. The pearls still reposed, unstrung, in a handkerchief. Grandma's emerald was contained in a little battered plush case. The black affair harbored sweet-smelling unguents.

Letty creamed her face, looking into the mirror which backed the cosmetic case. She removed the surplus cream with tonic. She laid herself a foundation. She pressed powder where powder was due, firmly, with large wads of cotton. She wiped it off. She made herself an enchanting mouth in the new bronzy-claret shade known as Siamese. She dampened a comb at the washstand in the corner and ran it through her curls. She was now ready for anything and anyone.

She took a current magazine from her suitcase and stretched herself out on the bed. She thought philosophically, Well, I needed the rest.

After awhile the magazine slid to the floor. Letty giggled. She giggled some more. She began to laugh. She was thinking of innumerable comic things: the expression on Miss Mehitabel Rogers's face, unsweetened lemonade; Judge Harvest's habit of twitching his nose like Peter Rabbit; the enormous dinner consumed by Constable Jones at her expense; David's face of warning and fury when she had risen to speak her piece . . . David's face —

She put her hand thoughtfully to her Siamesed mouth.

Presently she frowned. She'd make him pay, just the same. She'd have him fired. He could starve, for all she cared. He must starve. When he had starved himself into a state of sincere contrition and humility, when he came crawling to her on his knees she *might* ask Uncle Dick to take him back.

She yawned; and slept.

She was awakened from her nap by footsteps along the corridor. She sat up, a little chilly and considerably dazed. Where was Simpie, had the gang come, where was — everyone? Where, so far as that went, was she?

She remembered. She was in jail. Lights burned brightly in the corridor, the footsteps came closer, stopped before her cell.

"Well, little lady," boomed the deputy sheriff cordially, "hungry?"

Letty bounced to her feet. She replied, with simple appeal:

"I could eat a horse."

"You won't have to," said Mr. Masters, and unlocked the cell.

Letty looked at him. What, no tray? No bowl of mush and skimmed milk, no dry bread and water, no coffee composed of chickory?

He ordered:

"Come along to the house, the wife's waiting."

Letty said weakly:

"You mean I can go out?"

"Sure," said the deputy sheriff, "why not? Ruins good vittles to carry 'em over here. Wife won't hear of it. Lucky you came when we aren't busy. There's only one other prisoner, over in the men's cells. He's too drunk to care if he eats or not. I'll fetch him something later. Let's go, I'm hungry myself. You don't need your hat or coat, miss, it's just a step."

The Masters's house stood next door to the jail. It was reached by yet another corridor, a door opening to the crisp October night, a patch of lawn. Letty breathed deeply of the fresh cold air. You didn't know how much you'd missed your freedom, she thought soberly, until it was lost to you. To be able to breathe fresh air, to be able to walk more than a few circumscribed steps. Why, that was important, it really mattered! She was startled, thinking how much it mattered.

"Careful of that step," warned Mr. Masters, a large paw under her elbow, "always meant to fix the dummed thing, never got around to it."

They went in the shorter, back way. The big kitchen streamed with light, reflected from polished brass and copper. There was an odor in the air, heady and heavenly. A table was set for three, with a bright cloth and shining glass and silverware. Mrs. Masters was bustling around the stove. She was a little woman, brown as a wren. She shook hands with Letty as her husband performed the introductions.

"I'm glad to meet you," she said. "Set down. You must be starved. I thought you wouldn't mind eating in the kitchen. We're having the dining room repapered and it's a mess."

"I don't mind anything," said Letty.

"I declare," said Mrs. Masters, doing things at the stove, "it's a crime to put a girl like you in jail. But you hadn't ought to drive so fast. I always say that I'm glad John and I haven't any children, the way things are. It was always a great sorrow to us but when I see my friends' young ones, racketing around in fast cars and drinking too much and the girls going around in next to no clothes . . . well, perhaps it's just as well we didn't have any. I'd be worried clear out of my mind most of the time. I hope you like fricasseed chicken."

Fricasseed chicken, with yellow gravy and biscuits. Glasses of clear amber and pink apple jelly with a sprig of rose geranium leaf in it, amethyst grape jelly. More biscuits, fresh butter. Coffee, a miracle, and thick cream. A platter of cold ham, stewed tomatoes, lettuce salad, and a dozen kinds of pickles. And eventually a noble lemon pie . . . sweet as requited love, tart as New England wit, the meringue lighter than a child's heart, the crust as short as memory of debt.

When Letty had finished she looked at her empty plate with awe. She said sincerely:

"Mrs. Masters, that's the best meal I've ever had anywhere."

"That's nice of you," said Mrs. Masters, beaming, "and I suppose you've traveled a lot."

"Some," admitted Letty, smiling.

"Set still while I clear away. She don't have to go right back, does she, John? Of course not. Set there and tell us about it. Your travels, I mean. I always hankered to travel. Maybe someday we will. Florida now, that must be a nice place."

Letty asked, "Could I — could I smoke?"

"Of course," said Mrs. Masters instantly. "Not that I approve of it for myself nor wouldn't for my own daughter, but times have changed. Fetch her an ash tray, John."

Letty, replete, comfortable in the warm, fragrant kitchen, watched Mrs. Masters clear away. The deputy sheriff lighted his pipe. Letty leaned back and smoked her cigarette. She would sing for her supper. She would talk about her travels. She cleared her throat and began . . .

By the time the dishes were ready to wash, they were all old friends. Mrs. Masters washed and Letty dried, with a blue apron around her slender middle. Mrs. Masters thought she was too thin, and said so in kindly criticism. "If I had the feeding of you," she commented, "I'd fatten you up. How much do you weigh?"

"One hundred and four, dripping wet," Letty answered, "or I did before dinner. Shall I put these preserve dishes in the cupboard, Mrs. Masters?"

When they parted, "What do you like for breakfast?" asked Mrs. Masters. "John usually has cakes and sausages, or ham and eggs. But, of course, if you just take coffee, he can bring it over to you."

Letty said faintly:

"I usually take coffee, black, and fruit juice . . . but not tomorrow. Cakes, did you say?"

"Hot cakes," said Mrs. Masters.

"I'll be here for breakfast," Letty said firmly.

The deputy sheriff escorted her back to her cell. He carried an extra blanket and a hot water bag upon which his wife had insisted. Letty's feet might get cold, she said; nonsense anyway, sleeping over there, when there's a spare room, all ready, right here! "Good night," she said to Letty. "John will come and fetch you. You needn't get up as early as he does. And maybe you'd like to take a nice hot bath before you eat!"

The following morning, having slept like the dead, Letty was escorted back to the sheriff's and upstairs to the neat little bathroom where she wallowed happily in a tub almost too hot to endure. After which she went downstairs to pancakes, Vermont syrup, several cups of coffee, and several round little pats of sausage. Mr. Masters had gone his mysterious way but he would be back presently. She helped Mrs. Masters with the dishes, and said apologetically, "I'm giving you so much trouble."

"It's a pleasure to cook for you," said Mrs. Masters. "I like to have young people in the house. My sister's children used to come, holidays. But they're grown up and married now."

The last dish had been wiped when Masters came panting through the back door. He said, "There's reporters to see you, Miss McDonald."

"To see me?"

"Yep. A man from New Haven, and one from Danbury, and Mudd's been around and says that the New York reporters will be coming up too. Maybe you'd better get back to jail," he suggested, "it's more official."

Mrs. Masters untied Letty's apron and brushed a curl back of Letty's ear. She said, "Run along now, you look as pretty as a picture."

That was quite a day.

The local reporters, the local cameramen, the New York gentlemen of the press. The New York ladies of the press. Inez Robb, driving up, her hands encased in white gloves. Dorothy Kilgallen on her way to a game at New Haven, stopping off to greet the prisoner. Winchell didn't come, nor Chollie Knickerbocker, but they carried little items in their columns. And the headlines!

"Socialite Jailed."

"Society Gal in Hoosegow."

"Letty McDonald Samples Connecticut's Calaboose."

And such.

Miss Simpson came, a little anxious Simpson, a plump woman, with good brown eyes and a sensitive face. She brought a suitcase of fresh clothes. She wept when, the smoke of the photographers and reporters having cleared, she was ushered into Letty's cell. She said feebly:

"Yes, I called everyone up . . . they couldn't believe . . . they're all coming to see you. Oh, Letty, my dear, how *could* you do such a thing?"

"I didn't do it," said Letty crossly, her natural energy having flagged under the barrage of questions and the exploding flashlights. "That idiot David Alcott did it. Don't worry, Simpie, I'm fine. Everyone's marvelous to me . . . and I never ate or slept better in my life."

Simpie, sitting on the narrow bed, looked about her bewildered.

"I never heard of flowers in jail before," she said.

David's flowers. David's card inscribed painstakingly by the local florist from the message on the wire. "Just to lend a note of cheer to your surroundings and to wish you many happy returns of the day." Letty had torn it up. Then she put it together again. And she'd borrowed every available vase and empty preserve jar from Mrs. Masters.

"Neither did I," said Letty, "but then this is my first experience."

She hadn't been able to do justice to Mrs. Masters's noon meal what with the reporters and all, the said reporters having to be held in abeyance while she ate. Then Simpie came and after that the weekend guests, motoring up from town bearing files concealed in loaves of bread, baskets of fruit, a hymnbook, a phonograph and three records of "The Prisoner's Song." Messrs. Gage and Thomas assured her solemnly that they had tried to buy a pineapple but couldn't.

"But there's one in the basket," said Letty.

"The other kind. Blow up the jail and all that sort of thing."

They were personable, feckless young men. They thought it a great joke. Bibi Parker, a delicious blonde, was a little grave.

"Of course," said Bibi, "if you don't mind the publicity!"

"You would, wouldn't you, dear?" asked Letty sweetly. Bibi was her dear friend. She had never liked her.

Frank complained, "You ruined a good weekend for us, woman."

"Why?" asked Letty on an inspiration. "Go on back with Simpie, all of you, and have your delayed weekend. There's plenty to eat and drink . . . too bad to waste it."

"Marvelous idea," agreed Frank and Owen.

"We'll drink to you, darling," Frank assured her. "Come on, Simpie, let's go."

Letty saw them go with thankfulness and later attacked Mrs. Masters's remarkable supper with vigor and appetite. Mrs. Masters watched her fondly.

"Think of anything you'd favor for dinner tomorrow?" she asked, and added, flushing a little, "Letty?"

CHAPTER 6

On Monday morning Letty was packed and ready to depart. She had had a quiet Sunday. Masters had brought her the papers, she had eaten a superb and leisurely dinner, after which she combed and set Mrs. Masters's hair in a new style and one which became the little woman enormously. She had seen two reporters and Alec Kinney, who came to call and to offer his assistance if it was needed. She had had a nice long nap. And at breakfast Monday she spoke cheerfully to the deputy sheriff.

"I suppose I can go," she said, "right away?"

Mr. Masters looked glum. He shook his head. "Three days, Miss — Well, Letty, then. That makes it this afternoon. But I'll ring up Judge Harvest if you like and maybe he'll —"

"Of course he will," said Mrs. Masters, "he's not a fool; although," she added thoughtfully, "if he is my own cousin, on my mother's side, twice removed, he acts like one sometimes."

Masters came back from the telephone. He reported:

"The judge says you can go as soon as your lawyer gets here."

David! Her heart leaped, to her intense fury. She said, after a moment, "My lawyer . . . you mean Mr. Alcott?"

"Nope," said Masters, "that ain't the name. Tal— tal— something. Seems as if he telephoned the judge and said he'd be along for you before noon today and would it be all right."

Uncle Dick, said Letty to herself. David had telephoned him to let him know. She said, aloud, "You'd better lock me up again then, Mr. Masters."

She kissed Mrs. Masters good-by, and promised to come see her every time she went through Brookbury. "I don't know how to thank you," Letty told her.

Mrs. Masters colored engagingly. "I cut some of the pictures out of the papers. But they aren't very nice, don't do you justice. If you could spare a real good picture of yourself . . . ?"

"I'll have one taken," said Letty, "just for you."

She was sitting on her cot endeavoring to look forlorn when Masters unlocked the door for the last time and took her to the outer room where Richard Talbot was waiting for her. She had taken off most of her lipstick and her face was freshly powdered. But she looked excessively healthy. She had slept ten hours for three nights, as there was nothing else to do. She had gained almost two pounds.

She cried, "Oh, Uncle Dick!" and such was her mercurial temperament that she really did feel miserable when she saw him, penitent and unhappy.

He shook her hand briskly. He said temperately:

"All right, Letty, everything's been taken care of and we can go now."

She shook hands for the last time with the deputy sheriff and presently found herself and her suitcases in the big car. She spoke to Talbot's chauffeur, whom she had known for years, and he preserved an expressionless face in greeting her. But his eyes betrayed him. And there were quite a few people to see them go, including the indefatigable Mr. Mudd, who had procured a cameraman from somewhere and superintended a last shot of Miss McDonald leaving Brookbury's jail.

In the car —

"The papers played you up," said Talbot pleasantly.

"I couldn't do anything," she said defensively, "they just came swarming down like locusts. I suppose you're disgusted with me, Uncle Dick?"

"Well, no," he said, "not exactly. But it is too bad. You are old enough to know better, Letty. There's really no excuse for reckless driving or letting your license lapse."

Letty no longer felt penitent. She disliked being scolded. She said:

"It wasn't my fault."

"Whose then?" he inquired with a lifted eyebrow.

"Oh, I don't mean the accident. I mean the sentence. That was David Alcott's fault, all of it. He did it on purpose," Letty said angrily, "he could have got me out of it."

Talbot said reasonably:

"I talked with young Kinney this morning, and I've been to Judge Harvest's house. No, you can't blame it on David, Letty. He pleaded guilty for you, which was right and proper. I know exactly what he pleaded. If you had had sufficient common sense to keep quiet and not annoy the justice with reminders of the insurance company, if you had not adopted the attitude that everyone, constable, justice, and the lawyers alike were idiots — with, of course, the exception of yourself — you would, as you put it, have got off — with a warning and a fine."

She said crossly:

"David Alcott doesn't approve of me. He was glad this happened."

Talbot smiled.

"Suppose I try to interpret David to you. He's a very fine boy. He has worked hard all his life. His father is a country doctor. David always wanted to be a lawyer. He worked, summers, after school, in a law office. His father couldn't help him much financially, so David put himself through college and law school, by tutoring and by doing all sorts of menial jobs as well, and through earning scholarships. He didn't have much fun. He couldn't take part in the social activities, he hadn't the time nor the money. He couldn't join a fraternity. He couldn't play football although in high school he had been so promising that several universities wanted him. But he had to choose, you see, and he chose the Law. He loves it, and respects it. It is his life. Or shall we say justice rather than law?"

She said impatiently, "Oh, I've no doubt he's a model young man, Uncle Dick, an

Alger boy and all the rest, but that doesn't excuse . . ."

He said gently:

"Does he need an excuse? He did his best for you, Letty. He is not so constituted that he could offer bribes, even if he thought they'd be accepted, or lie you out of the jam you were in. He would not trade on your position or appearance."

"My appearance?" repeated Letty, shocked. "As if he'd notice!"

"Oh, he's noticed," said Talbot, smiling. "No young man could be exposed to anything so — so virulent, shall we say, and remain immune."

Letty said, "I told him I'd ask you to fire him."

"Ask away," said Talbot pleasantly; "that's all the good it will do you. I've been looking for a lad like David for a long time. He has exactly what I want in an assistant — or for that matter in a son. Character."

She said scornfully, "All work and no play —"

"But he *isn't* a dull boy," said Talbot gently, "he's an interesting one. He has humor, kindness, sentiment. Is it possible you have not discovered that?"

"What opportunity have I had?" she began.

"Plenty, I should think. Look here, Letty, try to be reasonable. You're a stubborn little thing and soundly spoiled. But perhaps that isn't your fault. You have too much money —"

"I'm broke," she said. "I tried to make your wonderful David get me an advance on my quarterly allowance. He wouldn't."

"Of course not. He couldn't even if he wanted to," said Talbot, sighing, "and you're always broke. You're not only extravagant, you're senselessly so. But perhaps it isn't your fault but that of your generation . . . idle, self-seeking and shallow. Often, I am afraid, unkind. And utterly unable to see that there is a law even higher than the laws at which it scoffs. A law of give and take, of retribution even . . . you pay for your fun, Letty. Haven't you learned that yet?"

Tears stung her eyelids but she kept her voice steady. She was fond of Richard Talbot, she respected him. She wanted his affection and his respect. She had always known that she wanted the former, today she was discovering that the latter was necessary too. She said presently:

"You don't know me, Uncle Dick, not at all."

Something in her tone touched him. He admitted quietly:

"Perhaps not. You dart in and out of my staid life like some brilliantly plumaged, exotic bird. How am I to know you?"

She said slowly:

"All my life I've been — shipped around. Left with people who were hired to watch me. Not Simpie . . . I do like her, Uncle Dick, really. But I've never been able to do what I wanted."

He said, "I thought you never did anything *except* what you wanted."

She said hotly:

"Nothing. I wanted a job. I wanted to learn to design clothes. I have a flair for it. I can draw. I wanted to go to art school and then to Paris to study. But Mother wouldn't hear of it, she thought it was absurd. It's too late now."

"Your mother . . ." he began.

She said, "You don't understand about her either. I was with her when it was convenient for her, that's all. When she needed me. You see, the money — I mean she had more when I stayed with her."

He nodded. "Go on," he said mildly.

"Last summer . . . that's why I'm broke. I said I'd borrowed from friends, I told David Alcott that, I said I wanted a new coat. It wasn't true. Mother needed money, she was in debt. She's so afraid of Freddie. Afraid she'll lose him, because she's so much older. So she keeps on buying him, going places he wants to go, giving him things. There's a girl in whom he's been interested. She told me about it, Uncle Dick. Abased herself. She — cried. It was terrible, seeing her like that. And it's always been that way. When I was little she wanted me with her because she could use the extra income . . . she'd snatch me away from camp, school, anything. I never had time to make friends, friends who would last, who'd matter. I'm not complaining, I'm just telling you the truth. When I was older she didn't really want me, because I made her seem older, I would be there to remind her how much older she was than Freddie. But the money counted. So she had me with her and kept me in the nursery. You know. Away from people, as much as possible. Simpie looked after me, we did things together. I hoped, then, that Mother and I — But she was always going places with Freddie, she hadn't time, she didn't dare have time, for me. And since I've been able to handle my own income . . . Last summer was pretty bad. She and Freddie quarreled continually. Then they'd make up. When they were quarreling, she'd come to me . . . then afterwards she'd forget me. She'd rather have me on the other side of the world, Uncle Dick, if she could manage without the money. She can write and borrow, of course."

She began to cry, suddenly, and Talbot put his arm about her. He said, distressed:

"I'm sorry, Letty. I never realized."

"I'm sorry too," she said with a childish gulp, "I didn't mean to make a scene like this."

That was it, he thought, understanding. Don't make a scene, don't show you're hurt, pretend you haven't an ounce of sentiment in you, be hard and careless and never let anyone know. His arm tightened. He asked, "Why didn't you come to me long ago?"

"It all sounds silly," said Letty, more evenly, "and besides it didn't make sense. To complain, I mean, to behave as if I couldn't take it. I used to hate the girls I knew at school whose mothers and fathers would come to see them, who had homes to go to, and people around them, their own people, who'd scold them and fight with them but who'd stand by and see them through, no matter what happened."

126

He thought sadly, That's it too . . . uncertainty, the lack of security, of continuity which family life gives. Poor little devil.

She said energetically, as if she had read his mind:

"I'm not sorry for myself, honestly I'm not. I've a lot more than most people. Money and looks, if they matter. And I have a good time. I've managed that. I shouldn't have told you about Mother and Freddie but something you said got under my skin." She leaned a little closer to him and the October sunlight shone on that flawless skin and dazzled her eyes and made her blink, like a child or a puppy. "It's just that everything's been so — so mixed up. Different schools, different camps, meeting people, getting to know them, losing them again. There was a girl I liked a lot. She had a raft of brothers and sisters and a big house and the most wonderful mother and father. It was a sacrifice to keep her in the school where I was, so after a year she left — she was going to take a business course and get a job. I wanted to leave too — and —"

"I remember," said Talbot thoughtfully, "you wrote me about it. Your mother objected very much and we decided —"

"Everything," said Letty, "was always

decided for me. Emily — that was the girl's name — wanted me to come and visit them that summer. I wanted to, terribly. But I went abroad instead."

He said, "You're free now, Letty, to study, to do anything you want."

She said, "It's too late. I don't want it, as much, not now. I've grown lazy, I suppose. Soft. Just as you said, I'm spoiled. I'm used to this crazy patchwork way of living, to not having friends who mean anything, to doing lunatic things. Poor Simpie, I've turned her hair gray. But she's — steadfast. This afternoon when we get back to town, she'll be waiting for me at the hotel. All the publicity will have worried her a lot."

"And it doesn't worry you?"

She said, "Not any more. It doesn't matter, does it?"

"I suppose not," said Talbot. "Letty, I'm sorry. I could have helped a great deal more than I have. But I didn't know."

She said, leaning back in her corner:

"It's not your fault. I'd feel like such a fool . . . I feel like one now. Misunderstood female. That sort of thing. It simply isn't done," she added, in her best British imitation. "I don't know why I spilled over like this."

He said, "I'm glad you did. You say

Miss Simpson will be at the hotel?"

"Yes; she drove to town last night with Frank and Owen and Bibi — I'd asked them up for the weekend, you know. Simpie phoned them not to come but they all arrived in Brookbury Saturday." She began to laugh. "If you could have seen the things they brought — I gave them to Mrs. Masters, she's such a dear, you've no idea how good she was to me — and then they went on to Rivermead. They said they'd drive Simpie down last night. The people who sublet the apartment are leaving — oh, you'd know that, of course — and we'll move in the end of the week."

He said thoughtfully:

"We'll have lunch, presently. And after that . . . I said I wouldn't go to the office till tomorrow but I've changed my mind. Will you go with me?"

She asked cautiously:

"Why?"

"I'd like you and David to be friends."

Her jaw set. She said:

"He doesn't want to be my friend."

"I think he does."

Letty was silent a moment. Then:

"If you don't mind, Herbert can drop me at the hotel."

Talbot sighed.

"All right, but hasn't anything I've said . . . ?"

"Of course, it has," she agreed. "I'm willing to admit that David Alcott's a model young man." The dimple near her mouth showed suddenly. "I'll go further and admit that he's attractive too."

"Would you go still further," asked Talbot gently, "and admit that he wasn't at fault on Friday?"

There was a long pause. And then Letty spoke in a small voice.

"All right," she said, "I admit it. But don't you dare tell him!"

Talbot began to laugh. He said:

"I'll let you tell him yourself. How about dinner, theater, and a night club some night this week. Just you and David and I — ? Say, Friday?"

Letty's eyes began to dance. She looked dangerous, he decided, regarding her with some trepidation. Yes, dangerous was the word for Letty. Poor David. Perhaps he was making a mistake in trying to patch up the differences between them. And such differences, of environment, heredity, upbringing, temperament, outlook! He thought, astonished, Why, they haven't a thing in common except their youth. But it was too late to withdraw the invitation.

"I'd love it," cried Letty, and flung her arms around him. "You're a darling."

He was strangled. He extricated himself. He could see Herbert's ears growing slowly red with repressed emotion. He leaned forward and said, "We'll stop at Silvermine for lunch, Herbert."

When Richard Talbot reached his office he was greeted by an amazed staff.

"We didn't expect you," said Lulu. "Mr. Alcott said —"

"I know. Is he in?"

"Yes, talking with Mrs. Lane. She's been here an hour, she'll be going presently, I imagine. Did you want to see her?"

"No, heaven forfend. Send Alcott to me when he's free," said Talbot.

He went into his office and stood for a long time at the windows, ignoring the mail on his desk. He was thinking of Letty. He was thinking, Perhaps I could have prevented . . . But he couldn't, he knew that. Not really. He had no jurisdiction over Rita Mott-Jordan who was, after all, the child's mother. He thought, But if I'd *understood,* there might have been a chance.

David knocked and entered, with unusual timidity. He said:

"Glad to see you back, sir."

131

"I'm glad to see you. I changed my mind . . . thought I'd come in for an hour today. Sit down."

When Talbot sat facing David across the big desk he said casually:

"I stopped in Brookbury for Letty."

David's face was scarlet. He said:

"I suppose she — ?"

"She's pretty sore," said Talbot, smiling. "But I think I made her see reason. We had quite a talk coming down. I don't know if her incarceration broke down her defenses —"

"According to the papers," said David grimly, "her incarceration was one happy holiday."

Talbot smiled.

"She's thrived certainly," he admitted, "and I imagine from what she said that it's due to the table the jail sets. Remarkable. As I said, we talked — and she's given me a rather different slant on things."

"Things?"

"Herself then. She's had a pretty difficult time."

David snorted.

"In Brookbury?"

"No," said Talbot, "I don't mean that. Listen, will you, for a minute." To himself he added, I was mistaken, they have something in common, after all. Stubbornness!

He talked of Letty, of her life, of her mother, watching David's face. It was grave now, and now it softened. When Talbot had finished, David commented briefly, "Poor kid."

"Yes. Not all her fault, is it? I hope it hasn't been mine. I didn't for a moment realize . . . I thought she liked her life, the skittering shallowness of it, like a dragonfly over a pond. But it appears that I was wrong."

"Me too," said David honestly.

Talbot said, "She's fond of me, I think. And of Miss Simpson. And she likes you," he added.

David's face, rapidly changing color, looked as if Picasso had been at it.

"*Likes* me? She detests me!"

"I don't think so," said Talbot. "She told me you were — attractive."

"Gosh," said David feebly, feeling rather like Edgar Bergen's bashful creation, Mr. Mortimer Snerd.

"And so," said Talbot, rising, "we three are dining and going to the theater Friday night. And," he added severely, "I expect you kids to —"

"To what?" David demanded, his heart extraordinarily gay. But he wasn't prepared for Talbot's answer, the common, familiar phrase which had grown meaningless through usage.

"To kiss and make up," said his chief.

CHAPTER 7

On the night of Richard Talbot's little party Miss McDonald wore a sweater and a skirt.

These are the bald facts of the case but when we embroider them with detail we see at once how misleading the most truthful statement may be. For Letty's sweater was whipped up out of yarn as soft as a kitten's ear, a baby's kiss, the pearly white of a floating cloud, liberally besprinkled — as clouds never are — with little golden stars. Her skirt was white, too, and to the floor, patiently pleated, knife slender, and on her hair she wore another starry cloud, y-clept a snood, and around her wrists and throat heavy barbaric gold bracelets.

David, not to be sneezed at in his evening garb — unless you are allergic to good-looking men — looked at her with awe. All she needed was wings.

Yet, when over the dinner table she regarded him with speculation and a dancing imp in each eye all she lacked was a pitchfork.

She said:

"It's a marvelous party, Uncle Dick, but you should have brought a girl for David."

Talbot answered comfortably:

"I was under the impression that I had."

"Who? Me, the fugitive from a chain gang? Me, the hardened criminal, slightly stir-screwy?"

"What's that?" demanded Talbot.

"Skip it, darling. It's the way jailbirds talk, you wouldn't know," said Letty negligently. "But it's tough on David — associating with gun molls."

David said, "I can take care of myself," and added, in a lower tone, "and you too, I think."

"You've certainly given me a marvelous demonstration," Letty said wickedly.

"Children," said Talbot indulgently, "this was to be a love feast, not a boxing match."

Letty grinned. She offered her hand to David. She said solemnly:

"All is forgiven. Or isn't it? I admit it was my fault. Shake, pard."

He shook.

Letty withdrew her hand and straightened out her fingers, one by one. She counted them anxiously, murmured, "I make it ten," and smiled at Talbot.

"Your young man hasn't lost his grip,"

she said negligently, "and I'm having a wonderful time."

"Finish your crepe Suzette," said Talbot, "or we'll be late at the theater."

On the way, he explained:

"Night life isn't for me. I fall asleep promptly at eleven. I've taken the liberty of engaging a table at the Hawaiian Maisonette for you two infants, the car will drop you there, take me home, and call for you again. If there's any other place you'd like to go, don't hesitate. Herbert has his orders and I'll let him sleep tomorrow. Satisfactory?"

"Perfectly," said Letty gravely, "I can hardly wait to hula with David."

"Sounds like a very good program," David agreed. He thought, Which will cost a fortune. Mentally he aligned his resources. Twenty-three dollars and eighty cents. How far would that take them? He had noted that, like that of many small, willow-wand girls, Letty's appetite was astonishing.

Talbot, however, had thought of everything. When they were leaving the theater he slipped an envelope into David's hand. He said, "My party, remember . . . and don't spare the horses."

He dropped them at the St. Regis and

drove off, smiling. The party had been extremely successful so far. They had enjoyed their dinner and had not quarreled seriously. They had liked the play. The rest of the evening was up to them.

He thought, anxiously, Am I matchmaking in my dotage? Still, it's an idea. Letty needs a lad of David's type, and she's a delightfully pretty creature, with more brains than I'd given her credit for, and since our talk the other day I have seen her in an entirely different light. As for David, Letty would keep him on his toes, and he isn't the type to be harmed by her money.

His better judgment warned him. They're entirely unsuitable, it said severely, and very antagonistic.

Mr. Talbot scorned his better judgment. He answered right back, Youth's never unsuitable and they'd adjust themselves . . . and a little antagonism adds just the right amount of spice to falling in love.

The Hawaiian Maisonette was enchanting. Letty and David had a ringside seat. Through the picture windows they could see the sky and the sea, Diamond Head and palm trees. The orchestra had Hawaii in its soul and the three hula girls were very pretty.

Presently Clara Inter came out and

danced while people laughed and applauded and a man who had been in Honolulu recently surrendered to her pleading and rose to dance with her.

"Makes me homesick," said Letty dreamily.

"For what?"

"Hawaii. Oh, you haven't been there, have you?" She regarded him with pity. "You must, someday."

Maybe it was the music or the champagne, maybe it was the memory of the love scenes they had witnessed on the stage, or just Letty herself, in gold and white with her dark curls vibrant with stars . . . maybe it was because he knew irrevocably that he was in love with her and had been ever since the day she walked stormily into his office. Whatever it was, he said:

"I'd like to — if I could be with you."

Letty gasped. She didn't blush because she never blushed. But she was conscious of very pleasurable excitement, quite different from any she had ever experienced. She retorted feebly:

"I bet you say that to all the girls."

"No," he said, "I don't. I never have. You believe me, don't you?"

She looked at him but her eyelids felt

139

weighted. She lowered them. She said, after a moment:

"Yes, I believe you, and it would be —"

"What?" he asked, leaning closer.

Letty said, as one who exorcises a spell:

"This won't do. It's the champagne or Uncle Dick's benevolent effect. We don't even *like* each other, do we?"

"Don't we?" asked David.

She sighed.

"Perhaps," she admitted. "Let's not talk about it, not now. I —"

"You what?"

She couldn't explain. She couldn't say, I like this uncertain state, nothing said, a good deal assumed, this sense of tiptoe expectancy, adventure round the corner. Let's leave it at that for a while. So she answered, instead:

"Let's dance . . . the floor's cleared now."

They danced. Maybe that wasn't such a good idea, after all. The floor gradually filled yet they were alone, revolving to heavenly music, very close together. He was so tall, he looked down on the star strewn curls, and bent his head to touch them with his check. They were soft and silky and he could not have lifted his head had his life depended on it.

More people came, people who knew

Hawaii. A pretty girl took off her shoes and sketched a small hula, very gravely, standing beside her table. Letty commented, laughing:

"There's something about Hawaii that makes everyone want to take off their shoes after midnight . . . I mean everyone who has been there."

"There's something about you —" said David.

"Don't say it," Letty begged him wildly, "or I'll break down and weep. What a brat you must have thought me, what a brat I've been! On Friday — was it only a week ago?"

He said, "You were adorable." He looked at her for a moment. "And I hardly know you. I don't know what you like or want or —"

She said rapidly:

"I like lots of things, gardens, sunsets, Lombardo's orchestra, Wayne King's and Duchin's. Everything Hawaiian except poi. I like oysters and one glass of champagne — more gives me a headache — and a cigarette after meals, and books and movies: Garbo, Bill Powell, Bette Davis, Gary Cooper, and of course, Donald Duck. I like swimming in very cold water, tennis in hot weather, golf in autumn. I like lots of snow and holly wreaths, Christmas trees and carols. And I want —"

"What?"

She said gravely, "I'm not sure. Perhaps I never knew."

"Listen, Letty," said David, "I haven't any right to ask you this — after all, I'm just starting out, on probation as it were —" his smile had a little boy appeal which set her heart to beating like a drum — "but, other men? There must be dozens of them."

She said, "Not the way you think. I fell in love when I was thirteen with the Prince of Wales. I never really got over that. I saw him, once. And later, there were movie stars. And when I was sixteen, a young Frenchman . . . he was going to marry his cousin, by the way, so that was that. There hasn't been anyone since, not really. Not since I grew up," she added, as if she were eighty. "Frank Gage is fun and so's Owen Thomas, but no girl in her right mind would take either of them seriously."

"Lots of them must have thought about you."

"Lots," she agreed. "Does that matter?"

"No. Shall we dance again?"

It was two o'clock when Letty said:

"We should go home. But there's a place . . . it's fun, rather. I've been there just once. It's quite new, they call it Tiger Den for no good reason. Let's go there for coffee and scrambled eggs. It's been such an evening," she added, sighing, "that I can't bear to have it end."

They left the Maisonette and went out to a cold, very dark night. Letty shivered a little and drew her coat around her. She said, "Last year's mink. I suppose I'll have to make it do?"

"I hope so, for quite a long time, and I hope that the next you buy —"

"Well?"

"How long would it take an honest young lawyer to earn enough to buy a mink coat?" he asked her.

Herbert was waiting for them, tucked them in, drove them to the Tiger Den. It wasn't far and traffic was light. But for a little while they were close together in the intimacy, warm and dark, of the moving car. Letty said contentedly:

"This is nice. I wish we were just going to drive . . . and drive . . ."

"Do you know what Mr. Talbot said," asked David, greatly daring, "when he suggested this party?"

"What?"

"He said he wanted us to kiss and make up."

"He's given us such a lovely party it would be a shame to disappoint him in anything, wouldn't it?" said Letty thoughtfully.

"That was exactly my idea," said David and put his arm around her. The car halted for lights and Herbert glared straight ahead of him. David bent his head and Letty raised hers. The result was instantaneous and eminently satisfactory. It was, as far as they were concerned, epoch-making.

The light changed.

Letty said quietly:

"Even with the bars between us, I liked it."

She moved a little closer to him. She said solemnly:

"David, do you honestly believe we're in love?"

"I am," David told her.

"Then I must be," said Letty, "I never felt like this before." She began to laugh. "It's absurd, it's crazy, it's wonderful. Let's not talk about it. Let's talk about it forever. Yet you couldn't possibly *like* me, David, I'm all the things you don't like . . . selfish and shallow and —"

He said tenderly:

"Maybe I'll grow to like you after a

while. I'm not concerned about that now."

The car drew up at the Tiger Den.

A bar downstairs and curious surrealist murals, definitely of the jungle. Upstairs a small room, a jungle orchestra, a lot of tigerskin upholstery, and a great many people. The headwaiter, definitely not of the jungle, came forward shrugging apologetically on recognizing Letty. He said, "I am desolate, Miss McDonald. There are no more good tables. Just one small one, against the wall."

"That will do very nicely," said Letty, and they went forward to claim the table. It was in a corner, and they had to sit very close and there wasn't much elbow room. Neither of them cared, as they didn't know where they were. They were alone, they were on a cloud, they were walking through a sunset, they were standing on a hilltop and the moon was rising. It takes some people that way. David was a Supreme Court justice, he was being groomed for the White House, he was district attorney, he was on top of the world. And Letty was sitting in the opera house with the lights down, listening to *Tristan und Isolde*.

Their hands touched, clung together. They smiled at each other, startled, uncertain, yet perfectly sure.

"Letty!"

"McDonald, the Belle of Brookbury."

"When did you get out of the big house, Toots?"

"Is that your new suit of clothes? I always understood they did well by you."

People, lots of them, waving, calling from the tables near by, stopping on the dance floor and coming over. The sunset faded, the moon set, the hilltop vanished and the great music. They were back again in the Tiger Den with a dozen of Letty's dear friends clamoring at them.

Bibi Parker cast an oblique turquoise glance at David and whispered loudly:

"Who's Handsome?"

"Meet my lawyer," said Letty, mistress of herself. "We'd ask you to sit down but there isn't room — just enough for David and me and Swenson."

"Who's Swenson?" demanded Frank Gage.

"My bodyguard. You can't see him. He's the Invisible Man," Letty explained.

"Yards of room in our house," said Owen Thomas. "Hey, Jacques," he shouted across the room, "three more chairs at my table."

"Three?" asked Jacques, disconcerted.

"One for Swenson, the Invisible Man."

"He can lie under my chair," said Letty happily. But on the way to the Thomas table she put her hand in David's. She said, "Sorry, darling," and smiled at him.

The Thomas table was noisy. There were others present, but no girl prettier than Bibi, with her long blond bob, her curly blond bangs and her frock of black velvet and lace. She sat next to David and he didn't hear a word she whispered, which was just as well. Eggs and coffee appeared and a drink for David, which he didn't touch. He kept looking at Letty, sitting opposite between Gage and Thomas, and didn't need any other form of intoxication.

The party grew louder.

A man came weaving across the room. He was a big man. He had a champagne bottle in his hand. He stood by the table and bowed to Letty. He said:

"Never saw you in my life. Think you're pretty. Know you're naughty. Read all about you goin' to jail. Some fun. How about a drink and a dance? Like little girls who go to jail. Like to be keeper of that jail."

He had glassy blue eyes. They leered. A lank lock of hair fell over his forehead. Gage said negligently, "Go away, big boy, this is a private fight."

David was getting mad. He was getting madder and madder. Letty looked the gentleman up and down, and turned her head away. The gentleman made a curious lunge across the table and caught her wrist. He said:

"Stand up and dance. Come on, be a sport."

Things fell over, things spilled, the table rocked. Bibi cried, "For heaven's sake!" and powdered her pert nose. Jacques started across the room, looking anxious.

"Let go of her!" ordered David, rising.

"Who says so?"

"I do."

Letty cried, "Sit down, David, do." Not to make a scene, not to take anything seriously in public, just laugh it off. She rose, with the man's hand still on her wrist. She said, "I'll dance, why not?"

"You won't," said David, and smote the gentleman firmly, smacked him neatly on the nose, bopped him one on the chin. Down went the importunate one and the bottle broke and foamed around him.

Chaos, Jacques, and two husky waiters entering the fray. Removal of the knight. Gage said reflectively, viewing the champagne, "Venus rising from the foam." Bibi shrieked gently. Everyone but David laughed and a columnist sitting drearily at a near-by table perked up, and began to take notes.

Letty said, "Really, David!" with displeasure.

"We're getting out of here," said David. "Come along, Letty."

"My," said Mr. Thomas, with admiration, "ain't he masterful!"

There was nothing to do but go. Letty vanished into the powder room with Bibi hard on her heels. She emerged, flushed with rage. David waited grimly at the foot of the stairs.

In the car, "You needn't," said Letty, "make a spectacle of yourself."

"The man was drunk, he got what was coming to him."

"I could have managed the situation," she said with dignity. "I could have laughed it off, or even danced with him, maybe. It's ridiculous to make scenes."

David said, "He had his hands on you. What were Gage and Thomas thinking of — sitting there, doing nothing?"

"You make them sound like a grocery firm. What could they do?"

"Plenty."

"Frank Gage," she said sweetly, "was

Princeton's star halfback not so long ago, and Owen Thomas held the heavyweight boxing championship of his university. They didn't sit still because they were scared! After all, things like that happen in night clubs and the sensible thing is not to —"

"Oh," he asked, "you've had experience, have you?" He glared at her. She had liked it! She had liked the noise and heat and silly chatter, she had liked the gentleman with the champagne bottle. He'd been mistaken in her. No, not mistaken. He should have trusted his intuition. The first time he'd seen her he'd known she was spoiled and —

They had reached her apartment house.

"Don't bother to get out," she said, and scrambled forth before he could move. She smiled at Herbert. "Thanks so much," she said pleasantly, "and I hope you catch up on your sleep."

To David she said viciously:

"Good *night!*"

Herbert slammed the door.

David opened it again. He was on the sidewalk. He cried, "Letty —" but she had gone.

Herbert said consolingly:

"I'll drive you home, Mr. Alcott."

"Thanks, I'll walk," said David.

"Walk!" repeated Herbert, stupefied. "But Mr. Talbot said —"

"To the subway, I mean," said David, and strode off furiously. Herbert looked after him. Love, decided Herbert, beat all. He grinned sympathetically. Hadn't Mollie led him a hell of a dance when he and she were four years younger? She'd settled down now. He'd like to tell Mr. Alcott that. They all settled down.

David didn't. He continued to simmer. The columnist had the story next morning. Others picked it up: Fracas At Tiger Den Club . . . Young Blackstone Bops Stag Line. Or words to that effect. Miss Letty McDonald, recently released from Brookbury jail is heroine of nightclub fight. Chivalry, said the columnist, isn't dead. . . .

It was bad enough to explain to Richard Talbot, who frowned at first and then laughed without moderation. It was worse to go into court on Monday and meet your erstwhile colleagues from the firm of Cather, Wilshire and Jervis, to say nothing of ex-classmates at the university, and get yourself unmercifully ribbed. Since when did earnest young lawyers go around smiting people hip and thigh in night clubs? Nice crowd you're mixed up with, my boy. . . . What will the Bar Association say?

That sort of thing.

He never wanted to see Letty McDonald again. He loved her, he despised her, she was shallow and silly, and she hadn't meant a word she'd said or a look she'd looked. She belonged in jail, to preserve sanity in society. She was at home in the Tiger Den . . . all claws, that girl was. She —

She came into the office on Tuesday morning and went in to see Richard Talbot. David wasn't there. But when he returned from court, his opponent having asked for, and obtained, a recess, he found her. Millie warned him. She whispered, "Miss McDonald's in your office."

He might have known it. He could smell the slight aroma of something heady and expensive all the way there. He flung the door open, he slammed it.

She rose from his desk. She asked faintly:

"You're still mad, aren't you?"

"Furious." He began to grin. There she was, all one hundred and four pounds. She wore something red, something hunter's green. She smelled like a garden, she looked like a flower. He repeated firmly, "Furiouser!"

"So am I . . . making an idiot of yourself and two of me!" She stopped. "Or were we idiots to begin with?" she asked in wonder. She advanced toward him, one hundred and four pounds of feminine determination. She no longer looked like a flower. She looked like a huntress. She asked gently:

"Kiss and make up?"

CHAPTER 8

That was the beginning, if the course of true love can be said to have a beginning. All that winter they went places together. They dined, they danced. Simple places. Letty took a charming new interest in the state of her escort's finances. Weekends, chaperoned by Simpie, they went to Rivermead and, as there was early, heavy snow, they skied and skated. She went to hockey matches with David, and she hated hockey. David went to the opera with her, and opera was merely a not too unpleasant noise to him. He shook his head over Tristan. "Why doesn't he die and get it over with?" he demanded. He viewed Crooks in *Mignon*, with alarm. "A big guy like that," he muttered as Mr. Crooks emerged from the burning building, "and he wears lace cuffs!"

They went to movies, they ate in the automat, they had fun. They went to Coney Island, which was completely deserted, on a bright cold Sunday and rode on the lone merry-go-round and watched the waves curl up on the shore. They went to the Zoo and fed the elephants and the monkeys.

They talked: of each other, of themselves. There was nothing in David's life Letty didn't know, now, nothing in hers of which he was unaware. They talked of the past and the present, but Letty wouldn't let him talk of the future. Not yet, she said.

He announced, "I won't live on your money."

"Darling, of course not."

"You can do what you want with it." He looked at her anxiously. "I'm selfish," he said with a groan, "I want to be everything to you."

"Aren't you?"

"Please God, I will be. Use the money for anything you want, clothes, fun . . . but for a while we won't be able to have —"

"Let's not talk about it, David."

"But you'll marry me, Letty?"

"No one else. But let's go on like this for a while . . . it happens only once."

"When, Letty?"

"Next autumn, maybe."

"Summer?"

"Darling, I don't know. I only know that this is what I want — now. For a little while. It will be different, after."

"Better."

"Perhaps. Of course. But now, let's just have this."

He had given her a ring at Christmas. A modest little ring. She loved it, she wore it — on the wrong hand. "Let's not be engaged," she said, "all that fuss and fury. Let's be like this and then, one day, we'll slip away and be married. No big wedding. No bridesmaids. No awful parties first, from which you emerge half dead, wishing you were. Just you and me, being married, and Uncle Dick and Simpie to stand by."

Winter slipped past, Letty wasn't going south this year. She was staying home, in the apartment with Simpie. David went there often to have dinner with them. He grew fond of Simpie and Simpie of him. Simpie said, privately, to Richard Talbot, "It's the best thing that could have happened. She's a different girl. She's so happy I'm frightened for her."

Talbot said cautiously:

"They quarrel?"

"Oh, twice a week," said Miss Simpson, "but that doesn't matter. They have an idea they must, I think." And then she said, smiling, "They're always reconciled."

March was cold and windy, snow-flurried. It was a very nasty month. And in March David and Letty, sitting together in her apartment, were arguing.

"But why not go to Rivermead?" she was saying. "There's still snow, and the pond is frozen."

"I know. But Sally and Victor want us, so much. You liked them, didn't you?"

"Of course," said Letty, "but I'm not a good guest. I mean —"

He interrupted earnestly, "Victor was a senior, my freshman year. He was swell to me. He married, as soon as he left law school. They haven't much, Letty, but they're so *darned* happy. I just want you to see how people who love each other, and who haven't money, live . . . all your friends have so much." He thought of the weekends he had spent with Letty's friends, on the Island, in Connecticut, in Bucks County. "This is different," he assured her. "Let's go, darling, this once."

Victor Remsen was a lawyer, a clerk in a big firm, a pleasant, attractive young man. His wife, Sally, had worked in the advertising department of a big shop before her marriage and had gone on working until little Victor was born. Since then the small Janet had come along. They lived on the Island and Victor commuted. David had taken them out to dinner once, to meet Letty. The girls had got along very well.

Sally was thin and dark and smart, chic without being pretty. And they'd had a lot of fun. Out of that evening this invitation had come.

"All right," said Letty, "love in a cottage." She tilted her head and smiled. "I'll see your sample," she said.

They drove down to Sunnybay on a windy, showery, sleety Saturday morning. Victor had the day free. He was waiting for them at the picket fence when they drove up. He wore an old windbreaker, an old hat, and corduroys. He shouted at them, cheerfully.

Sunnybay was a real estate development, a lot of houses, none of them alike, a little pond which dried up in summer, a bumpy road leading in off the main road.

Victor's house was white frame. There were no trees around it yet, except the small straggling cedars. In summer a rose vine grew upon it but it was not in bloom in March. There was a little covered entry cluttered with roller skates, and a screened porch to the left opening off the living room. Victor ushered them in, insisted on carrying the bags. He opened the door and shouted for Sally. The hall was small, three steps led down to a good-sized living room with a fireplace. The fireplace had a fire in it. It was smoking. Sally was poking at it and turned to greet her guests. She rose, looking smudged. She said presently, "Vic, the damned thing's smoking again."

"Draft open?"

"Of course, stupid."

"Then the chimney must be wet."

All men like to monkey with fires. David was no exception. He proffered instant, expert assistance. Sally took Letty's arm. She said, "I'm so glad you could come, I'll show you your room."

It was a pleasant small room, very chintzy. Sally said apologetically, "There's only one bath, I'm sorry."

"Never use more than one," said Letty cheerfully, shedding her little mink turban and her coat.

Sally picked up the coat and stroked it. She said, "It's wonderful. Vic promised me one, a long time ago. We even had some money put by — but then we bought this house. You see, little Vic has sinus trouble. Town wasn't good for him."

"May I see him?" asked Letty.

"He has a cold," said Sally, "I have to keep him in bed. He's in our room. I put David in his. David won't mind, he's a lamb." She smiled at Letty. "You're lucky."

Four small bedrooms. Letty had the

guest room, David had little Vic's, Janet had her own tiny place. They went in to see her, a rosy child playing with blocks. Janet was three. She said, with dignity, "I'm hungry, mummy."

She lunched with them, royally condescending from her high chair. She spilled the milk, she upset a vegetable dish. She was not disconcerted.

After lunch the men went out for a tramp and Letty stayed with Sally and helped with the dishes. Sally said, "I get bored stiff with it sometimes. I was never much of a housekeeper. I want to go back to work, I could get my old job back and make enough to have a good maid. But Victor won't hear of it. You know how men are." She put a dish in the cupboard and said savagely, "I haven't had a new dress for a year, I need a perm, and I'd sell my soul for a course of facials. But we've had to be careful. Little Vic had his tonsils out last month, and Janet was awfully sick in the autumn. Things go that way."

That was a long afternoon. Little Vic needed attention and his mother scurried up and down stairs. Janet came with her toys and played contentedly at Letty's feet. Letty wasn't very used to children, she hadn't a natural gift of entertaining them.

Janet wanted something, Letty couldn't understand her, there were tears. And presently Sally had to start dinner.

The men came in and sat around the fire, reminiscing, talking of old days, of men they had known. Talking of the present, of cases, of things that were Greek, Latin, and Sanskrit to Letty. Presently she excused herself and went upstairs. There wasn't time for a bath because Sally was bathing Janet and after that something happened to the heater and the water wouldn't run hot.

Letty dressed and came down for dinner. She wore a simple, long-sleeved dinner frock. Sally looked at it with envy. She was enveloped in an apron. She said, "You don't mind if Vic doesn't dress, do you? I told David not to."

The soup was scorched and the meat overcooked. That was little Vic's fault, calling from upstairs with five-year-old imperiousness. He wanted this, he wanted that. He was hot, he was cold, he was sleepy, he was wide awake. He had developed a cough and worked it overtime.

Sally wouldn't let Letty help clear away. The talk around the table was desultory, with Sally jumping up in the middle of things to remove plates, bring others.

"Stack 'em," said Victor, "we can tackle 'em after. Dave and I stopped in to see the Petersens, they're coming over."

Sally looked at him. She cried, "Oh, why, Vic? You know they always want to be amused, contract, drinks. We can't afford their stakes."

He said uncomfortably:

"Dave hasn't seen old Pete since they were at college."

David said hastily:

"I'm sorry, Sally. Vic didn't suggest it, Pete did — they have people there for the weekend."

"How many?" asked Sally. Letty could see her counting, in her mind.

"Three, I think, a girl, a couple of men."

The Petersens and their guests arrived presently. They were a hearty, noisy crew. Two bridge tables were set up. Sally vanished to get out the ice and the bottles.

Letty didn't like contract much, neither did David. They looked at each other with commiseration. They played with the Petersens, the stakes were fairly high, the Petersens very good. Also, they quarreled, over the hands.

In the middle of the game Janet created a diversion by creeping downstairs in her woolies and being adequately sick in the middle of the floor.

Before the Petersens left it was after midnight. Letty had no time alone with David except at the door of her bedroom. She reached up and kissed him. She said, "We haven't had a word —"

"I know. Tomorrow —"

Tomorrow.

Letty didn't sleep much. Little Vic coughed. Janet was sick again. There was a procession to the bathroom. Her room was next to Sally and Victor's. She could hear them talking, through the thin walls. Once she thought she heard Sally crying. She couldn't be sure.

She couldn't sleep in the morning either, because Janet, quite recovered from her indisposition, came waddling in at six, and got up on her bed. She said, "Let's play house."

That was fun, rather. A cuddly, rosy little girl playing house, building it of blankets and quilt. They were laughing uproariously when Sally came in. She looked white and tired. She snatched Janet from the bed and Janet howled.

"Bad girl, waking Letty up." She smiled wanly at her guest. "I'm so sorry. You must have been awake half the night, what with the goings-on. We tried to be quiet."

163

"I didn't hear a thing," said Letty gallantly.

She jumped up, slipped into the bathroom when there was an opportunity, washed hastily and collided with David, in his bathrobe, when she came out. She clutched her thin robe around her and said airily, "Fancy meeting you here!"

"Start the day right," he said, and kissed her before anyone caught them. His woolly robe made her sneeze. They parted, a little breathless.

After breakfast, after the dishes were washed, Letty went walking with David and their host. It had cleared to a windy blue day. They tramped over back roads and she listened to the men talk. She felt a little forlorn and out of it. She was glad to be back in the house again, offering to set the table for Sally.

"Where are the finger bowls?"

"We haven't any," Sally said, after a moment. "We don't run to them, yet."

Oops! said Letty to herself. It seemed to her that Sally had fixed her with a hostile eye. She said cheerfully, "Good, I hate the things myself, always in the way, as unnecessary as an appendix."

No matter what she said, it was the wrong thing.

Dinner was on the stove and the kitchen was warm. But the house was cold. There was something the matter with the furnace. Victor went down to the cellar and came back, apologetic. He had forgotten to order oil.

"Well, of all the fool things," said Sally, brushing a wisp of hair from her flushed cheek, "and little Vic with a cold!"

"I'm sorry, Sally."

"You're always sorry," she said; "it doesn't do any good."

"I'll call them first thing tomorrow."

"Meantime," asked Sally, "we can freeze to death?" Her voice broke and she ran back into the kitchen. Letty said brightly, "Have you heard this one . . ."

The story wasn't so funny, after all.

Dinner wasn't too bad. The peas were hard and Janet wouldn't eat her sieved carrots. But somehow they got through with it. And after dinner Sally washed the dishes and Letty dried them. And Sally advised urgently:

"Don't marry a poor man, Letty."

"Why not?" asked Letty. "Lots of women have and have liked it."

"Is that a crack?" Sally demanded.

"No, of course not, I just meant —"

"You don't mean anything," said Sally.

165

"How could you? You've plenty of money of your own." She shivered. "You'd better put on your coat or something, this house is like an icebox. I'm glad I put little Vic in bed. I'll have to put Janet to bed too, and she'll raise Cain. She hates her nap and when she discovers that she can't get up after it, well —"

Later in the afternoon David and Letty found themselves alone for the first time. Sally had gone up to the children and Victor was off somewhere trying to get oil. He'd thought of a place open Sundays but the telephone hadn't been answered, so he took the car and went to see for himself.

Letty and David sat on a shabby sofa in front of the fire which David was keeping up. It still smoked. But they were content, just sitting there, with Letty's head against David's arm. They heard Victor come in the back way and go down to the cellar. They heard him come up the back stairs, you heard everything in that little house.

"Let's go out and get some air," David suggested, "my eyes are full of smoke."

They went hand in hand to the hall where they had left their outdoor things that morning. And then they heard the voices. They didn't dare move, for they knew instantly that Victor and Sally must never know that they had heard.

". . . I don't care," said Sally, "it's just like you. Asking people down here when we aren't equipped to have them."

"But you said it would be all right. You said you could get old Eva in."

"How did I know she'd get the flu Friday night and that I'd have to do the work? Cook and slave and make beds. And finger bowls! Your glamorous girl friend wanted to know where we kept the finger bowls. Well, we haven't any, or any gold plate either!"

"She isn't my girl friend," said Victor reasonably.

"She's David's, isn't she? And you're David's pal. Men are wonderful, the way they don't see each other for years and then suddenly remember what buddies they were in the good old days. I'm sick of entertaining your friends!"

"What about yours?" he demanded. "They aren't so hot. How about your dear little school roommate who came for a weekend and got so stinkin' drunk we had to send for the doctor?"

"That's right, throw that up to me, it wasn't my fault. Who got her drunk? I didn't. You were soppy about her, purring over her, wanting to turn up the rug and dance."

He said, "Pipe down, they can hear you."

"I don't care if they do. I'm sick of it, of cooking and scrubbing and being up nights with the children. I'm going back to work. I'll hire a maid. I'm too young to look the way I do. I look forty, my hair's a mess, my nails look as if they'd been run over with the lawn mower. As if we didn't have enough trouble, you have to get big-hearted and invite people down."

"It's my house!"

"Who saved so you could pay for it?"

He said, "Women are all alike. Want to be carried on a silver platter. My mother had six kids and did all her own work and I never heard her complain."

"That's right, hold your mother up to me as an example!"

"*Will* you keep your voice down? Or do you want David and Letty to hear?"

"I don't care!"

She began to cry, and Janet, hearing, raised her voice in a yelp and little Vic began to cough and scream.

"Good God," said Vic in desperation, "it's a madhouse!"

"You can just look after them for once,"

said Sally. "I have to get supper for your buddy and his million-dollar heartbeat. Finger bowls!"

Two doors slammed.

David looked at Letty. Letty whispered: "We've got to get away from here, and the quicker the better."

"How can we?" he asked helplessly. "We were supposed to stay for supper."

But she was running upstairs, singing happily and loudly, she was in her room, she was packing, and David followed slowly.

Sally came into Letty's room, pink-eyed but calm. She had powdered her nose, she had rouged her lips.

"Packing?" said Sally. She flushed. She asked quickly, "Were you downstairs just now?"

Letty made wide eyes.

"We've been out walking . . . just came in. I hadn't an *idea* of the time. We'll have to rush!"

"But aren't you staying for supper?" asked Sally.

"Supper?" Letty whirled around. She said contritely, "That David! He told me — Oh, men are the limit. I'd made an engagement for a cocktail party. I hadn't the least idea you wanted us, Sally, we'd *so* much rather stay here."

"Can't you change your minds?" asked Sally hollowly. Two more insincere females were never together in the same room. David could hear them. He marveled, terrified at the duplicity of women.

Half an hour later they were on their way back to town. David was driving Letty's car.

"Well," said Letty on a long breath, "if that's young married love in a rose-covered bower, I don't want any part of it."

"That's unreasonable," said David; "things just happened to go wrong."

"You can't tell me that they just went wrong because we were there!"

He said, "Letty, you've told me over and over again that you're afraid of marriage because it doesn't last. Half your married friends are divorced and remarried. That didn't mean anything, back there. Vic and Sally will stick together."

"I should hope they would. Who else would have them? Of all the bad-tempered — And Sally's no manager, she —"

"Could you manage," he asked, "with things the way they were and a couple of kids, one of them sick and —"

"I could not," said Letty, "and I certainly don't intend to!" She set her little jaw. "You're always telling me that half the trouble with my friends is that they marry for money. Well, maybe so. If that's marriage for love which we just witnessed, give me solitary confinement!"

CHAPTER 9

The car swerved, Letty shrieked. The car righted itself and David said:

"Okay. That lets me out, I guess."

His tone was singular. It was glum and stiff, stuffed-shirt and melancholy. It resembled nothing on earth except, perhaps, too much cornstarch. Letty said promptly:

"If that's the way you feel about it!"

They were on the highway. He could not pull off, silence the purring engine, and argue. He drove on erratically. After a while he spoke. His words were pebbles flung into a cool, still pond with a coating of ice upon its surface.

"It can't always be like that," he said, and the starch was gone from his voice. "There are just times when things go wrong. We happened to hit one. You're too intelligent to believe that marriage — any marriage — is a long sweet song. There must be days when the notes are sour." He drew a deep breath. "Everything's all right now," he said confidently, "want to gamble on it?"

"How?" asked Letty cautiously, but her eyes brightened. She was a born gambler.

"We haven't been gone more than half an hour," he said, "and we haven't a date for cocktails. We can go back to Vic's and see for ourselves; just sneak up and take a peek in the windows, maybe."

"Suppose they aren't where we can see them?"

"We'll ring the bell."

"Then what do we do, master mind?"

"We say you left something, go in and look for it and you'll find it in your handbag, after all. Your pearls," he suggested vaguely, "or Grandma's emerald. It doesn't matter. I'll say, all women are idiots."

"You would," said Letty. "All right. Let's go."

It was two miles before they could turn off, make a circle and head back to Sunnybay. They were rather quiet. Once Letty giggled.

"What's funny?" David asked her.

"Nothing. Keyholes. Looking through windows. I feel like a Broadway columnist."

"If," said David, "what you see satisfies you, will you retract your recent statements on marriage?"

She answered, as they turned off the highway:

"You think I'm a coward — don't you? — a putter-offer. Of course, you do. But what I've seen of marriage scares me, David. What — what we have is darned near perfect. I can't bear to lose it."

He reminded her gently:

"We fight. We just did."

"But it doesn't mean anything," she argued, wide-eyed, moving close to him.

"Perhaps Vic and Sally feel that way," he suggested.

She asked:

"And if you find Vic with his throat cut and Sally with her neck wrung — and I wouldn't be a bit surprised, thank you — what will you do then?"

"Call the police," replied David cheerfully.

They had come to the turn which would take them to Victor's. David pulled the car off the road, turned off the engine. He said, "Come on, we'll walk the rest of the way; they'd hear a car."

He helped Letty out, locked the car and, hand in hand, they started down the road. There were ruts, half frozen, and places where the mud oozed under their feet. Letty was retaken with a fit of the giggles and had to stop. David said severely:

"Looks like you'd found a tee-hee's egg in a ta-ha's nest!"

She stopped dead and stared at him. It was dark, cold, and windy. She cried, "David Alcott, what on earth does *that* mean?"

"I wouldn't know," he admitted happily; "my mother used to say it." He caught her to him, bulky in her furs, and kissed her cold face and the end of her nose. He let her go, laughing. "Come on," he said.

They circuited the path, they crept up to the porch, and stood there peering through the glass into the living room beyond. A fire burned on the hearth and there was no longer evidence of smoke. Victor and Sally sat on the big shabby sofa. Janet in a woolly robe, was curled up in Sally's lap and little Vic, wrapped in a blanket, was sitting beside his father. They were talking and laughing. As David and Letty watched, they saw Victor bend his head to touch Sally's hair with his cheek. She looked tired, and happy. After a moment she rose and dumped Janet in Victor's lap. She said something, smiling, and vanished.

"Gone to get supper," deduced Letty, whispering.

David caught her hand and drew her

away. They trudged back toward the car. He said:

"Well, no blood, no cut throats, no police. Disappointed?"

"The little house," said Letty slowly, "it looks — just right, doesn't it, with the lights shining out and the four of them, safe, inside?" She stopped and threw her arms around him. "And I do love you, David," she added.

In the car, on the way back, "You didn't say I told you so," she reminded him.

"Why should I? You could see for yourself."

She said, "I suppose they're lucky, fights and all."

David drove in silence. Then he said:

"They're just average, Letty. Given the breaks, they'll come through with flying colors. The happy marriages don't make headlines. We hear only of the unhappy ones. There are millions of people just like Vic and Sally, struggling along. Of course, they fight. Two people can't live together, day in, day out, and not fight. It wouldn't be human. But they love each other, they have a — a sense of continuity. I see a lot of the broken marriages in my job. I might grow pretty bitter about it only I've seen so many of the other kind too. In the town I came from . . . where you knew all your neighbors."

"You win," said Letty.

When April came, with her false, pretty smile, her sudden tempests, they went back to Rivermead as often as David could get away, walked through the wet woods and tramped on the muddy roads. In town, Letty shopped furiously for new clothes and refused invitations to go south to Virginia or the Carolinas. She and David had settled down. Miss Simpson was a little alarmed. Weeks would go by and there would be no excitement. She didn't like the look of it. Was Letty getting bored?

But in June when she and Letty moved back to Rivermead for the summer — "You'll come every weekend," Letty told David, "and I'll come to town often, darling" — things began to happen. David was kept in town several times and had to make his peace. And once Letty came to New York unexpectedly, went straight to the office from the train, and found young Mildred weeping on David's shoulder. Neither of them had heard the telephone ring to announce Letty's arrival.

That took some explaining. Letty looked in, and flounced out. Mildred had wept harder than ever. "Oh, Mr. Alcott," gasped

Mildred, sniffling, "what will she think?"

"What do you think she'll think?" asked David grimly.

He had a hard time catching up with Letty. Luckily, he had no appointment for an hour. He chased her through the office, just missed her elevator and caught her in the revolving door downstairs. He shook her, there in the lobby, for everyone to see.

"Don't be a little idiot!" he cried.

She said, with dignity:

"Office wife stuff. I might have known. Never trust a blonde!"

David explained wearily:

"It's her boy friend. They've quarreled. She was a little on the dumb side when she took my letters this morning and I spoke to her somewhat sharply. Then she began to cry. I don't like seeing women cry."

She said, "Let me go, I have a date. I only came down to see the dentist. I thought I'd surprise you. And I did. I thought we could lunch —"

"We can. I'll meet you — at one."

"You needn't bother!"

He met her, she wouldn't eat, her tooth ached, and she glared at him. He went over the entire business until he lost his voice. And finally said hoarsely:

"All right, I give up. Only when she

brought me the letters to sign and I found that she had written 'Oh, Frankie darling, how could you?' in the middle of one I had dictated to a vice-president of the National City Bank, naturally I had to take steps!"

"Did you have to take 'em toward her?" demanded Letty.

"Damn it, Letty," said David, "Millie's a good kid. And I was sorry for her."

He relapsed into gloom and stared at his plate. Suddenly, miraculously, Letty's tooth ceased to ache. She smiled at him brilliantly across the table and said gently:

"All right, angel, I forgive you."

"Forgive me?" he began, and then subsided. He knew when he was licked. He promised humbly: "Well, it won't happen again." Privately, he thought, You're darn tootin' it won't, not if I have to have a little chat with Frankie himself about it!

Toward the end of June the uneven tenor of David's love life and the even but increasingly interesting routine of his work were interrupted. Mr. Patrick Morrisey came suddenly into his present, and thus affected his future, in a major way. Yet up until that hot sticky day David had never heard of Mr. Morrisey.

Richard Talbot heard of him first. He received a call from Police Headquarters which informed him that one Patrick Morrisey of such and such an address was being held in durance vile on the charge of drug smuggling and, having stood firmly upon his innocence and statutory rights, had demanded to see his lawyer. Whereupon with an incredulous expression, Mr. Talbot answered the call and went to see his client.

When he returned he sent for David and went into the details.

"Pat Morrisey," said Talbot, "is a goodhearted, likable gentleman whom I've known since he was a kid. His mother was my cook, and a good one. She cooked for me for twenty years, after which I pensioned her. Pat lived with his aunt and her husband. He was always in a scrape but never in a serious one. He might borrow a dollar but he'd never steal it, and anyway he always meant to pay it back. I used to spend a good deal of time getting jobs for him. He drove for me for awhile, he was a good chauffeur, reliable and sober. Not that he didn't drink, but only on his days off. Then he married, and about the same time had trouble with his eyes. I found him a job as a packer in a shipping firm and he was there for years. Last autumn he lost his job, the firm went out of business. I finally got him a berth down on the docks, he's been there ever since. He's married to a nice woman, and has three kids."

Talbot pushed a box of cigarettes across the desk to David, and went on:

"And now you're wondering what this has to do with you."

"Go ahead," said David. "What happened?"

"A few hours ago a freighter came in from a South American port. Pat was on the docks. The ship carried a few passengers. Pat happened to be near the gangplank when they disembarked. A man came down the gangplank, followed by a ship's steward carrying his bags. The man carried a small square package. He beckoned Pat, handed him the package, and disappeared before Pat could say a word. Pat, according to his story, yelled, 'Hey, mister,' and started running after the man. But he had vanished in the crowd and the steward too. Pat gave up, and stood there, dumb, turning the package over in his hands. Whereupon a couple of detectives marched up and took him into custody. The package contained drugs."

"And you mean to tell me . . . ?"

Talbot shrugged.

"I believe Pat," he said. "He's never been

mixed up in any racket, let alone this one. He's a decent fellow. I don't say that he doesn't get drunk now and then. He gets into fights too; I've bailed him out more than once. But he doesn't steal, he doesn't lie, about things that matter, and he definitely is not on the receiving end of a dope ring. He told me a straight story. I'm inclined to think that either this man mistook Pat for the person to whom he was to give the package, or else — and this is more likely — he caught a glimpse of the detectives in the crowd and simply shoved the evidence into the nearest pair of hands. I've had a long session at Headquarters. They're questioning the crew, they've got a squad searching the ship. All the stewards are accounted for and the man who carried the luggage isn't among them. He was simply a man in uniform, I fancy . . . and not a member of the crew. Pat's description of the passenger is vague — tall, dark, middle-aged. He wouldn't know his voice, as he didn't speak. Of course, the passenger list's available, yet I don't think they'll discover anything."

David asked:

"You really believe in Morrisey's innocence?"

"I'd stake my reputation on it," said his

superior, "and I want you to go into court and prove it."

"Me?"

"You. This is a young man's job, David. Have you any idea of the proportions drug smuggling has reached? The district attorney's office is after 'em, tooth and nail. They've made some convictions, done fine work. But it isn't over yet. These rackets aren't like the old ones, David. You're up against very different types from the old-time criminals. There are plenty of brains behind such an organization and it *is* organized, and to the nth degree. Lawyers, doctors, businessmen . . ."

"Sure, I know."

"A dangerous outfit," said Talbot, frowning. "Just now we aren't concerned with them except as they've affected Morrisey. You know my schedule. I'm up to my neck. I must be in Chicago next week, and in San Francisco the middle of July. This is up to you. See Morrisey, and talk to him. Headquarters will round up our passenger. They'll find him, all right, but he'll produce a clean record . . . I'm certain of that. Meantime I'll arrange to have Morrisey's family taken care of."

"Bail?" suggested David.

"It's a very serious offense," Talbot reminded him; "besides Pat will be safer in jail than out. Especially if he knows anything. I don't think he does, but others may. Jail's the place for him, David, until he's tried and acquitted."

"Whoops, let's go," said David, his eyes eager. This was a tough assignment, something you worked to get your teeth into; a change from corporation law, accident and divorce cases, from getting people out of the hands of moneylenders, and all the rest. His last appearance in court had been dull, a technical squabble about a real estate title. This meant going places.

He was permitted to see Morrisey, who first regarded him with suspicion but soon warmed to him. Pat was a stocky, smiling redhead, the smile a bit subdued at the moment. He couldn't understand, not at all.

"I'm standin' there, mindin' my own business," he told David, "and up comes this guy and shoves the package in my hand. I looks at it, dumb, see. Then takes after him, yellin' like a banshee. But he isn't there. He's gone. And up comes the flatfoot and claps his hand on my shoulder."

David asked:

"You've been working around the docks

for some months now, Pat — ever seen anything like this before?"

"That I haven't. Of course, there's talk —"

"Talk?"

"There was Anderson," said Pat, thinking hard, his forehead creased, "he was a big, hulkin' guy, the kind you see on the docks. Hadn't had a job for a long time, glad to get that one — hardly enough in his jeans to pay the union dues. After a bit he gets hold of some dough. He took to flashin' a roll and talkin' pretty big, sayin' there was more where that came from. Maybe he talked too much. Anyhow, they found him in the river last March . . . verdict was, overboard while intoxicated."

"Did you ever see anyone give him a package . . . when a ship came in?"

"Not me," said Pat. "Wait a minute . . ." He thought furiously. After a moment he said, "Maybe I did. I couldn't swear to it, but it seems like I seen — No, I couldn't swear to it — out of the tail of me eye, it was." He looked hopefully at David. "You've got to believe me, Mr. Alcott, I wouldn't get mixed up in anything like this, not if I was starvin'. I've got the wife and kids to think of. Besides . . ." He lapsed into silence, his good-humored round face grave and resentful.

"Besides what?"

"I had a sister," said Pat with an effort, "did Mr. Talbot tell you? No? I suppose he wouldn't, at that. She was younger than me, pretty as paint. Where she first got hold of the dirty stuff I don't know. They had her over on the Island a couple of times. She's dead now, God rest her soul. I wouldn't touch the stuff, Mr. Alcott, and that's a fact . . . not for *no* money!" He swore steadily under his breath.

David said:

"Okay, Pat, I believe you."

He was very busy after that. Headquarters had questioned all the passengers. Their records were clear. On the list were three men answering to Pat's description, "dark, tall, middle-aged." Two were South Americans, one a native New Yorker. All were respectable businessmen. And when the time came Pat couldn't pick one out from the others and identify his man. After all, he'd had the merest glimpse of him. It was raining, the sticky hot rain of sudden summer, the man had worn a raincoat, and a Panama hat was pulled low over his eyes. He had, Pat swore, a mustache. These men were clean-shaven, two had worn raincoats, and all of them had Panamas.

The room steward swore that none of

the three had worn a mustache during the voyage. No one else had noticed. It had been a rough passage. Two of the men had kept to their staterooms.

David took to going down on the docks and talking to the men who worked there, who hung out there, and to the policemen. He talked to the taxi drivers. Headquarters had combed town for the taxi drivers who had met that ship, had found them all, had them up for questioning, but their stories checked with those of the passengers they had carried. None of them knew anything of any value to David's case.

He turned Pat Morrisey inside out. When he was through there was nothing he didn't know about him. He talked with Pat's priest, a quiet man with farseeing eyes and a slow, contagious smile. He talked with the tradesfolk in Pat's poor neighborhood and with the neighbors. He assembled enough character witnesses to enable Pat to run for president. He went to see Mamie Morrisey and sat for hours with her in the little cold-water flat, with the gas jets hissing on the landing and the children and cats and dogs on the stairs.

Most of the time he didn't see Letty. He was too busy to go to Rivermead weekends. Now and then she came to town and he managed dinner with her, lunch, tea . . . an hour snatched somehow.

Being with Letty was light after darkness, gayety after gloom. But, also, it was difficult.

"But why can't you? For heaven's sake, David, I expect you weekends and then you phone at the last minute that you can't make it. So I mooch around by myself or fill up the house with people who bore me stiff. What's so important? You aren't in court, you can't be so occupied!"

He explained, as best he could. A man in whom Talbot had been interested for years, falsely accused on a serious charge. Talbot looked to him, David, to see things through for Pat Morrisey.

He said earnestly:

"If you think I like staying in town . . . when I could be with you — You don't know how I want to ditch the whole business."

"But what can you do on Sundays?" she wailed.

"I see people, I talk to them: working people, people I can see only after work or on Sundays. I tell you," he said, his young face stern, "I've got to get Pat off."

"All right, David." She smiled at him suddenly. "You will, I know it. And after that — wouldn't Uncle Dick give you a vacation? You rate it, darling, and I miss you so much."

"Of course, he will," said David, and put out his hand to cover hers. "And I miss you — haven't I told you so, over and over?"

"Funny little scraps of letters. I'm saving them, for our grandchildren," she said, without blushing.

He said:

"It may often be like this — after we're married. Almost as bad as being a doctor's wife, Letty. And the older I grow, the more weight I carry in the office, the worse it will be. Taking trains and planes, off to get depositions, to interview people, to see clients. I'm warning you!"

She said:

"All right, I'll take up knitting."

He glanced at his watch, beckoned a waiter, looked at Letty, cool as a lettuce leaf in a green linen frock. She was going back to Rivermead in half an hour. He'd rather go with her than do anything in the world. But he'd been tipped off, early this morning. Not for nothing had he bought drinks for the men on the docks, not for nothing had he helped that independent driver with the ticket. He knew now where he might find the steward, the one who couldn't remember that any of David's three suspects had worn a mustache on the trip, the steward who had jumped ship and hadn't sailed back to the home port.

He said:

"You don't know how I hate this — but I've got to go, sweet — and pronto."

She said, sighing:

"All right, David, call me, will you, when you have time?"

CHAPTER 10

The D.A.'s office was very much interested in the Morrisey case. It was of vital importance that even the lowliest members of this ring be caught — and made to talk. But Morrisey was represented by Young David Alcott, of Richard Talbot's office, and young Mr. Alcott produced so many character witnesses and so much plain, logical argument, coupled with real eloquence, that it looked very much as if, after all, the watchful gentlemen on the docks had made a grave mistake. Moreover, Mr. Alcott had a surprise witness, one he had not been able to track down until just before the trial.

The ship's steward.

The ship's steward, who admitted that he hadn't seen anything very wrong in swearing to the fact that a man was clean-shaven, not if he was well paid for it. Five hundred bucks, just for that.

The dragnet went out for the tall dark gentleman from South America, who was a respectable businessman dealing in fine coffee, whose papers were superbly in order. But he wasn't around any more. He had left, rather hurriedly, for Canada, when no one was looking, despite the fact that he'd been asked, politely, to stick around please until the trial was over.

A slip-up somewhere. But no fault of David's. He hadn't procured his information until the last moment, and had in no way obstructed justice.

What amazed the D.A.'s office was the fact that, while working on the Morrisey case, Mr. Alcott had familiarized himself to a very great degree with certain angles of the drug-smuggling business. He had gone into it, as far as possible in his private capacity. He had statistics and data. It all came out in his defense of Morrisey. And he proved as well — which was more to the point — that Morrisey had been, in very fact, an innocent bystander.

"It could have happened to any of us," said David gravely, "for I am convinced that the gentleman who is now somewhere in Canada was either apprised of the fact that detectives were waiting on the dock, or else saw them. Even had the right person been at hand to receive the package, he would not have done so. No, Morrisey must receive it, utterly unaware of the dynamite it contained. It's an old trick and a good one. It's been done a thousand times before. Which is just too bad for the Morriseys of this world."

When Morrisey was cleared of the charge against him, to walk out, a free man, back to Mamie and the kids, David wired Talbot. He was as triumphant as only a young man who has accomplished a tough assignment can be. He also was a free agent once more. He was free to go to Rivermead for the weekend, free to call Letty and tell her so. And more than anything else he was free of the terrific burden which would have laden his conscience had not Morrisey been cleared.

That night he went out to dinner. He went to the Morriseys' and Mamie had cooked a chicken for him, with dumplings. The kids were shining-scrubbed and in their best, even the baby in the rickety high chair. And Father Dennis came to dinner too and Pat's old mother, in from the Long Island village where she lived on Talbot's pension, and where David had visited her of late, and Pat's uncle and aunt came, and there weren't enough chairs or plates but the neighbors supplied all deficiencies. And after dinner the neighbors came in and there was talk and a good deal of praise and glory, for David. And he'd never spent an evening he enjoyed more.

Also, he and Father Dennis, between them, had a new job for Pat, a janitor's job. A flat went with it, with hot water and heat. So the Morriseys would be moving, the first of the week. It wasn't too safe, David thought, for Pat to be on the docks any longer. His eyes might be sharper now. If he saw anything, he'd tell. If he told, his number was up. So David went to Father Dennis and they put their heads together, and the new job was found.

In August things were pretty quiet at the office. Richard Talbot was back, living in his old salt-box house in Connecticut. Lulu Randolph returned from her vacation and Mildred was about to go on hers. David was to have a vacation too — two weeks, at Rivermead. But he and Letty spent the first weekend of it with Talbot.

"You'd better be proud of this boy, Letty," said Mr. Talbot, "he's done a very good job."

"I am proud of him," said Letty, "but I hope he doesn't have too many of them."

"So you can't take it?" suggested David.

"Of course, I can take it. I didn't understand about it, though, until Uncle Dick explained, until I read the papers. But that's dangerous, David," she said gravely, "and I don't like that."

"Well," said Talbot comfortably — "pour me a glass of sherry, will you, Letty? — it's not often that we have such cases in a staid old office like ours, so I wouldn't worry. From now on David won't be exposed to anything more perilous than a pretty blonde looking for a divorce."

"I think I'd almost prefer the Morrisey type," said Letty, sitting back in a deep old chair and looking with satisfaction around the pleasant, book-lined room. The long golden shadows of evening lay on the lawn and a robin sang from the elm near the window. She said, smiling, "Let's have a place just like this, David, someday."

"What's wrong with Rivermead?" demanded Talbot.

"Nothing. Yes, there is. It isn't lived in enough. I just — use it. You understand? But this place . . . there's something about it."

"I don't live in it much either, these days," said Talbot; "and as for Rivermead, when you and David really decide to get married . . ."

Letty said, "David says it's too far from town."

"All right," said Talbot. "Put it on the market and when you're married I'll give you the salt box for a wedding present. It's too big for me — I used to fill it with people but I don't any more. So I'll give it to you on the condition that I may come up sometimes and use the southeast bedroom. Is it a bargain? Letty, for heaven's sake, don't strangle me!"

At Rivermead, Letty and David swam, played tennis and golf, and drove over to dance at the nearest country club. They quarreled a dozen times about nothing at all. David had ideas about bathing suits and he said he could put Letty's in his pocket. After it was off Letty and dry he demonstrated, and Letty told him he was twenty years behind the times. They bickered over that for a while until it grew too hot and iced tea appeared on the lawn, and fresh cookies. They quarreled over Frank Gage too. Frank came to dinner and decided to stay the night, having driven over from a house party twenty miles away. Dull people, awful food, worse drinks. So he stayed and David lent him pajamas and such. And after dinner he repaid this kindness by getting a little tight and instigating a game of tag . . . with forfeits. He caught Letty, claimed the forfeit and, as he was very close to the river, David threw him in.

It was all very healthy and invigorating.

David had almost forgotten the Morrisey case. Morrisey hadn't, nor his wife nor his mother nor the neighbors who had raised David to the position of a minor patron saint. David didn't know it but from now on when anyone in the old neighborhood, or for that matter in the new one, fell into any kind of trouble — be it a drop too much taken, or a good hearty private fight, or a little matter of dispossessing, or simple breaking and entering — David was going to be called. If you took on a Morrisey you took on his family and his friends. Talbot had known this for some time, but David was to know it to a far greater extent.

Another thing that David didn't know was the upset in the D.A.'s office. One of the good men, the very man who had been most interested in the Morrisey affair, since it came under his jurisdiction, was ill. He had a serious operation and then complications, after which a long convalescence was indicated, and in addition to the rest prescribed by his doctors for purely physical healing, he needed a longer time in order to heal his nerves. For he was a fighter and a doer, and he had been overworking, as it was his nature to overwork. And when the D.A. himself went to see the doctors he learned that his assistant should not be back in the office again for at least six months and possibly longer.

There was gloom in the office over that, gloom because of Mac himself, whom they all liked, and gloom because of the spot his absence would put them in. Financially Mac was all right, he had an excellent income of his own. He was an answer to a D.A.'s prayer, or to anyone's for that matter, a crusading, hard-hitting man, with a capacity for taking infinite pains, a genius for work, and so much money that salary didn't matter. He wasn't looking for experience, waiting until he was sufficiently ahead to set up in his own practice. Mac wanted to be just where he had been in the D.A.'s office, doing the hard routine work that doesn't make headlines and getting results. Sometimes the results were spectacular and made headlines, but Mac wasn't interested in that. He just wanted to do his job, and his make-up and situation were such that nothing could turn him from it, no proffer of advancement, no hope of preferment, no corrupt dream of wealth.

Mac's department included investigation into the smuggling of opiates and narcotics. A tough department, a pet of the D.A. himself, a baby, a favorite. And Mac's departure was a serious matter.

They were in the D.A.'s office one day, a handful of them, and a man who had been assigned to the Morrisey case under Mac's direction said after a minute:

"That kid who got Morrisey off — he's a comer."

Mac had spoken of "that kid" more than once. Mac had taken David out afterward, found a quiet corner, bought him coffee and a sandwich, and they'd talked it over. Mac had said later that he'd wished he had him on his side of the fence, and admitted, "It wasn't being clever — not that he isn't smart enough — it was his absolute conviction that Morrisey was innocent. Hell, he convinced me halfway through the proceedings."

"What's his name?" asked the D.A.

He was reminded.

"Firm?"

Someone remembered that.

The D.A. looked thoughtful. He said:

"Talbot's an old friend of mine. I might have a talk with him."

Which is how it happened that a day or so later the D.A. was sitting in Talbot's office.

"Well, Mr. District Attorney?" asked Talbot, smiling. He knew this dynamic young man well. He had campaigned for him, he called him by his first name.

"It's about David Alcott."

"What about him? Step on your sacred toes?"

"No," said the D.A., grinning, "nothing like that. He was right, and we were wrong, worse luck." He rose and wandered over to the window, his hands jammed into his pockets. "If during my incumbency I could break this damned drug ring, I'd die happy. We've laid the groundwork. Mac's a wonder, as you must know. But Mac's out of the running for a year."

Talbot remembered Mac. He remembered him as an undergraduate of the law school of a great university. Those were the days when Talbot lectured there and he could see Mac now, sitting in the front row, his eyes intent, his slight body tense.

"Out of the running?" he asked in dismay.

The D.A. explained.

"I see," said Talbot. Then he added, "Well, come to the point. What do you want of me?"

"Alcott," said the D.A. "We want to borrow him for a while. Until Mac comes back, at any rate. Unless he wants to keep on with us, if it works out that way."

Talbot said quietly:

"I have other plans for him. He's a good boy, and a worker. He's been here less than a year but he's fitted in. He doesn't make mistakes. He's willing to learn and he never passes the buck. He —"

"If it's salary, of course," interrupted the D.A., shrugging.

Talbot said mildly:

"I'm not paying him any more to start with than you would. That isn't it. He'll get a raise as time goes on. He'll get one this fall, he's going to be married. In, say, three years he'll have a junior partnership and a share in profits. And when I retire he'll have as much of my practice as he's able to hold. I think it will be plenty. Mind you, anything may upset this. I don't know. But I don't believe it. I think David will go on as he's begun. And if he does — well —"

"The sky's the limit, eh?" said the district attorney. "Lucky stiff. I could find it in my heart to envy him."

"I don't think so," said Talbot. "You've just begun to hit your stride. None of us know where it will lead you, although there have been rumors."

The D.A. grinned. He said:

"Look, if Alcott agrees, would you lend

him to us for, at the most, a year? It may not be that long. Say Mac comes back in eight months, even six? But during that time your kid would be gaining invaluable experience."

"And I," said Talbot, sighing, "I go back to the grindstone?"

"You won't mind," said the D.A., "you'll like it. I never saw you look better, you old fraud."

"That's so," admitted Talbot. "Saw my doctor the other day. Arteries like a schoolgirl's, if schoolgirls have arteries, blood pressure like a baby's, heart like an ox, lungs like a bellows. I get tired now and then, but that's all."

"You've been malingering," said the D.A., "talking of quitting at your age!"

"Who said quit?" demanded Talbot. "I didn't."

"Of course not. Well, can we borrow him?"

"It's up to the boy," said Talbot. "He's off on vacation, with a few more days to go."

"We need him now," said the D.A.

"All right, steam roller," said his friend, "I'll telephone him to come to town. I hope you can keep his fiancée out of your office," he added thoughtfully, "because she'll give you more trouble than anything you've got on file there at the moment."

The D.A. departed and Talbot rang for Lulu. He was used to talking things over with her. Sometimes he wondered why he hadn't married her. He was very fond of her. He'd never been in love with her, of course, but — He'd been in love just once in all his life.

"Lulu," he said, "sit down. I want to talk to you about David."

When he had finished, she nodded. She said:

"It will be experience for him . . . I think he ought to accept. Of course," she said, smiling, "he's no longer a free agent."

"You mean Letty?"

"Whom else?"

"Nonsense," said Talbot, "she wouldn't stand in his way."

"That's all you know about her," said Lulu, "about most girls her age."

"Well," said Talbot, "we're not getting anywhere. Except that I'm glad you agree with me. David must decide. I'll call him tonight when he's likely to be home."

Letty and David were lying in long chairs on the lawn. The river flowed smoothly below them, and there were stars in its dark waters. Behind them the lamplight flowed like another river from the house. There was a faint smell of roses. Far off on the main road the traveling lights of cars went by. Simpie was somewhere in the house, and beside them the coffee grew cold on the glass table. They had had a good swim and a better dinner. They were happy and replete.

Letty's frock was white cotton lace. Her hair was bound back with a red ribbon, there were red sandals on her feet. She said lazily:

"I've never been happier."

Simpie called. "David — telephone . . . David!"

David said, startled:

"What in the world —"

"Find out," suggested Letty. "You know. Go up to the house, pick up that funny black thing, put it to your ear and listen. If it's business, hang up."

She went with him, her long skirt whispering on the grass. The grass had been newly cut. The smell of it was enchanting . . . at least to two young people who were in love and who had no truck with hay fever. Simpie wasn't in love and she had hay fever. She was sneezing violently when they arrived at the house. She said, muffled:

"Id's Mr. Talbod."

"You sound like the elephant's child," said Letty sympathetically.

When David finally replaced the telephone on its cradle, Letty was dancing with impatience. She cried:

"What is it? I couldn't tell. All you said was yes and no and really and of course. What's the idea, growing stenographic in your old age?"

He said blankly:

"Look, darling, I have to go to town tomorrow. The district attorney wants to see me."

"Lud," said Letty, "whatever have you done?"

"The Morrisey case," began David.

"Oh, that. I'll drive down with you," she said, "and do some shopping and we'll come back together."

He said, frowning a little, looking from her to Simpie:

"As I understand it, the D.A.'s office wants to borrow me for a while."

"Borrow you?" asked Letty, incredulous.

"For a year," he said, "or perhaps less. To work with them on certain investigations . . . Mr. Talbot's made an appointment for me."

"You mean," asked Letty, "that you'd

leave Uncle Dick and go into that office and get yourself all mixed up with criminals and —"

"That's about the size of it," he admitted.

"You're crazy," said Letty, "throwing away your future. I'm surprised that Uncle Dick even suggested — I never heard such nonsense!"

He wasn't listening. He said, "I think I'd like it."

"You'd never have time for me," said Letty, "it would be the Morrisey case all over. You march right down there tomorrow and say you won't do it."

"Suppose I want to?" he asked slowly.

Miss Simpson stood by, holding her breath. She sneezed. She had to. She blew her nose and waited. Neither knew she was there.

"You're ungrateful," cried Letty, "after all Uncle Dick's done for you! To desert him like that. If you do," she concluded furiously, "I'll never forgive you!"

CHAPTER 11

Letty turned and ran out of the house toward the terrace. David turned to Miss Simpson and signaled with his eyebrows. She said pacifically:

"It's probably Mr. Talbot's fault. He's been telling her for months now how well you are doing, what great plans he has for your future."

David said:

"That's all very well. But she's utterly unreasonable. After all, this suggested appointment is in the nature of an — an honor, isn't it? And it isn't forever. It won't hurt my future; if anything, it will help. Not that I've made up my mind, I'll have to talk to Mr. Talbot and the district attorney first."

Miss Simpson twinkled slightly.

"You've made it up," she said, "just because Letty has made up hers. You're two excessively stubborn young people. Heaven help you when you're married."

"You needn't worry," said a choked voice behind them, "it's not very likely that we'll ever be married."

They turned. That was Letty with stop-flags flying on her cheeks and her hair as disheveled as if she had been pulling it.

"Letty," began David, and took a step forward, but she was already halfway up the curving stairway. From the upper regions the sound of a door slamming reached them all too clearly.

"That's that," said David hollowly.

"She'll feel differently in the morning," Miss Simpson assured him soothingly.

He managed a grin.

"Thanks, Simpie," he said, "but I've an idea this is serious."

"Not any more than usual," she suggested hopefully. "You'll see."

He patted her shoulder.

"Thanks," he said again. "Well, I'm for bed. I'll get an early start tomorrow."

He had his car now, a modest one which he had bought recently and of which he was inordinately proud. A scratch on its shining fender afflicted him, a dent sent shudders up his spine. He was sentimental about that little car. It took him galloping over the roads to Letty.

He slept badly that night, trying to think things out. Talbot hadn't said much, merely explained briefly. He'd have to weigh it all, very carefully. And he must make Letty understand.

If she'd been at breakfast . . . But she wasn't at breakfast. Miss Simpson presided over the coffee urn. She said, "I'm sorry, David, she won't come down, she says she has a headache. Perhaps, when you come back —"

"I'm not coming back."

"But your vacation isn't over."

"As far as I am concerned," he said, "it is."

Lack of sleep, his own slight headache, a problem which he couldn't share with the person who mattered most because of her peculiarly obdurate nature — these things shattered his perspective. Simpie said warningly:

"This isn't the time to do anything foolish, David."

She'd said as much to Letty. Letty hadn't slept either. When Simpie sat down on the foot of Letty's bed a little later and said brightly, "Well, he's driven off, in a cloud of dust, bag and baggage, and he isn't coming back," Letty retorted, "Good. And see if I care!"

"Of course you care, my dear," Miss Simpson said gently.

The fortunate sun streamed into Letty's room, a turquoise and cherry room with gleaming old maple, wide floor boards, and lots of books. Letty sat up in the four-poster. She wore a sprigged nightgown of mull and lace and a bed jacket to match. Her black curls were tied with a cherry bow. She had set her breakfast tray aside. She looked slightly wan, definitely defiant, and very, very pretty.

"Why are you so set against David's accepting this appointment?" asked Miss Simpson.

Letty said, "If he'd talked it over, if he'd consulted me . . . but no, he had to make up his stupid mind — like that." She snapped her fingers.

"He had very little time to consult you. I don't think he *has* made up his mind. He'll have to talk over the offer with Mr. Talbot."

"Uncle Dick's besotted about him," said Letty bitterly; "he'll say he approves no matter how he feels."

"But what in heaven's name," demanded Simpson, taking rare courage, "have you against it? It can't be the money. I know very little about these things but I imagine that his salary would be equal to that which Mr. Talbot pays him — money's never bothered you before, you've enough of your own to supply any reasonable lack. It —"

Letty said, "It's silly, that's what it is. He was all set. Uncle Dick told me not long ago that it was a matter of just a few years before David would be a junior partner."

"That still holds," said Miss Simpson patiently; "this is only a temporary arrangement."

"Suppose he likes it so much that he won't go back to Uncle Dick?" demanded Letty. "And he might, you know. He had more darned fun running his legs off in this Morrisey case. Suppose he wants to keep on with that sort of thing, then what?"

"He's taking another man's place," began Miss Simpson.

"But they could find some other pigeonhole for him," Letty told her, and Miss Simpson shrugged.

"Would that be so dreadful," she inquired, "if it was what he wanted? After all, David has his career to think of, Letty, and it's very important."

Letty said, after a moment:

"I knew a girl once — she was older than I, a swell person — I liked her. Her husband had some sort of job in the district attorney's office and I give you my word she *never* saw him. He was always breaking dinner engagements, he'd be away days at a time, she could sit and stew in the country, summers, all by herself. It wasn't much fun."

"You're arguing yourself into this, Letty," said Miss Simpson. "You don't mean it and you aren't as selfish as you pretend and you're really in love with David. Or aren't you?"

Letty burst into tears. She said:

"Oh, go 'way."

Simpie went, closing the door quietly.

David detoured, before reaching town by way of the sleepy village which contained the Talbot salt box. He found Talbot puttering around his roses, cursing mildly. He had a tin of gasoline into which he was dropping the rose bugs.

"David! I didn't expect you . . . I thought —"

"I'm on my way," said David. "Look here, Mr. Talbot, what do you think about all this?"

Talbot sighed.

He said, "I've grown used to you. I'll miss you. But it won't be for long and if it appeals to you, David, I'd take the offer." He straightened his back and groaned. "What does Letty think?"

"How can she think," demanded David dramatically, "and with what? She's against it from the word go. Not that she knows anything about it!"

"It isn't necessary to warn you," said Talbot gravely, "that the job is dangerous. I am not exaggerating. Perhaps Letty thought of that."

"She hasn't any idea," said David; "and what's more, I wouldn't tell her. I'm not going to trade on that."

Talbot said, smiling:

"You and Letty have differed before. I wouldn't let this worry you. Sit down on that bench and relax. We'll have an early lunch and you can make your appointment easily. Meantime, we'll have a chance to talk. You can telephone me later, after your decision is made." He brought his hand down hard on David's shoulder. "This experience will be good for you, I think. You won't get anything like it in my practice, nothing closer than an occasional Pat Morrisey. And your name stays on the door of your office. We'll all be waiting for you to come back."

David remembered this — indeed, he was never to forget it, nor the grave, friendly eyes, the assurance of affection — as he sat in the district attorney's office and listened to what he had to say.

"You realize what you'd be up against?"

the D.A. asked him. "The groundwork's been laid. We've made numerous convictions, but not enough. This isn't spectacular, Alcott, it's slow, underground and often very disheartening. It doesn't work out as things do in mystery novels . . . When the office does something dramatic it isn't a spur-of-the-moment affair, although the headlines make it look that way. It means months, even years perhaps, of work. You'll have help, the special detectives assigned to your department, other attorneys —"

David said, "I should think they'd resent a new man. After all, they've been in this a long time."

"They won't resent you," said the D.A. "Mac was the heart and soul of this job. If anyone can fill his shoes you can, despite your lack of experience. The way you handled the Morrisey business proves that, the way you went about getting your information."

David said thoughtfully:

"I think I can get more where that came from. I made a few friends during the course of that case."

"It's only fair to warn you," said the D.A., "that Mac had his bad moments. Twice someone took pot shots at him.

There was a time when he wouldn't let any of the lads from the office walk with him on the street. Think that over, Alcott, before you say yes."

David grinned.

"I'm all over goose bumps," he said cheerfully, "and that's not kidding. Pot shots! Good God! But it wouldn't matter . . . I mean so far as my decision is concerned."

"Good," said the D.A., "glad to hear you're scared. Haven't much use for a man who says he isn't. Either he has no imagination or he's lying. And imagination is sometimes necessary. Can you handle a gun?"

"I was brought up in the country," David said, "and I've been a whiz with an air gun in my day and later with a shotgun and a rifle. I'm fair with a revolver."

"You'll need one," said the D.A., "and a license to carry it. By the way, Mr. Talbot mentioned the fact that you were engaged to be married. I think that you should talk this over with the young lady. She might have something to say about it. You see, unfortunately, after you're sworn in, you won't be in a position to talk things over with her. And you'll be pretty busy." He laughed, his dark eyes cordial. "Some girls," he said gently, "resent a man's job interfering with his social life."

David shook his head. He said, with much more confidence than he felt:

"I'm not worried. Letty will understand."

The next few days were chaos. David was sworn in as assistant district attorney. He was licensed to carry a gun and he bought one, feeling like one of the Rover boys. He moved from Brooklyn. His brief residence created no snag, he had been there less than a year, had not voted there, and prior to his removal across the bridge had lived in Manhattan. Now he returned to Manhattan, taking a small flat in the Village. Lulu and Mildred helped him move. Mildred reminded him tearfully that when he returned to the Talbot office she would not be there. Someone else would practice her Gregg to his dictation, for Mildred and her Frankie had made up their dispute and were to be married in the autumn. David thought, astonished, *And so am I . . .*

Was he? He hadn't heard from Letty. She wouldn't come to the telephone, she wouldn't reply to his letters. Simpson wrote instead, in her genteel sloping hand: "She's sulking, David, be patient, she'll get over it."

David moved into his own office in the grim building which housed the D.A. He sat up nights going over files. He had long smoky bull sessions with the special detectives and the other men assigned to him. He assimilated things quickly. He worked, at home, until the small hours of the morning, poring over reports and documents, in his shirt sleeves, an eyeshade casting a sickly pallor over his intent face, a big ash tray overflowing with odoriferous cigarette butts beside him. His sole companion was a lean black kitten with a white waistcoat, white boots, and a pink nose, which had adopted him. David took him in, fed him, named him Conscience — Con for short. Con curled up on a chair beside him and washed himself devotedly while David worked. Occasionally he sang.

That was a hot month, all thirty-one days. September was hotter. The Village steamed and the office steamed and all the places David went were not rose gardens. He spent much time at Headquarters looking at unpleasant pictures, reading unpleasant dossiers. He was present, in the background, at line-ups. He spent a good many hours over on Welfare Island, listening to the incoherent, horrifying monologues of white, shaking creatures who had been deprived of the drug by which they lived.

One evening he came home, tired. He and one of the special men, Ryan, had been out chasing ghosts. They had been to some unsavory places. The day before they had made a raid and their net had caught a couple of the smaller fish. Nothing startling, but the little fish lead to the big ones. Because of information gained after this fashion, he and Ryan had stepped out together for a gentleman euphoniously called Mopey. They had not found him.

David opened the door of his flat. He had not eaten since noon. His head was fuzzy from smoke and bad air. He was also discouraged. Not that he had expected to land anything worth shouting about in the first weeks of this assignment, but there was so much plodding routine to the business, so much to learn.

His little living room was well lighted. The center of the radiance was Letty, sitting in the leather chair, with Con in her lap.

"I just dropped in," she said airily.

It was like falling in love all over again. He had known that he had missed her, terribly, he had known that this longest alienation was heartbreaking, but he hadn't known how much he'd missed her, and how hurting heartbreak could be — not until he saw her sitting there, smiling at him.

"Well, say something!" she said impatiently.

"How'd you get in?"

"I told the janitor I was your estranged wife," she said brightly.

He made a mental note. Talk to janitor. Not even Letty should —

She made a quite hideous face.

"Not glad to see me?" she began. "Chivalry — Oh!"

He had picked her up, purring cat and all, he had kissed her as if it were for the first time, or the last. Then he sat down, with her in his lap.

She said, "I'm sorry I was —"

"Keep quiet," he said, "forget it."

After a long time she said plaintively:

"I'm hungry."

David put her on her feet. He said, "So am I . . . we'll eat." He bent down to stroke Con who was much offended, disturbed in his cat nap. "Sardines," he promised, "to celebrate. We'll bring you some, old boy."

Letty was looking around. At the books, the pictures of herself, the littered desk. She said:

"I like it here . . . let's live here when we're married."

"When's that?" demanded David.

"First," said Letty, "let's eat."

A good Italian place, clean, wonderful spaghetti and ravioli, and a fair bottle of wine. A fat gentleman, the proprietor, rather like Letty's favorite movie character, Mr. Armetta. Smoke, a low ceiling, murals of Italia in impossible blues and greens, and not too many people. You put a nickel in the slot and a phonograph played.

She said, "You're thin, you look tired."

"This is work, believe me." He smiled at her happily. "I like it."

"Tell me about it."

"There isn't much to tell," he said cautiously. "I've a lot to learn. What have you been doing?"

"Missing you. Writing letters and tearing them up. Coming to town now and then. Bibi Parker's back. She's got the oddest man in tow, a Brazilian. He's staying with them at Great Neck. They drove up to see me and I spent half an hour washing my hands afterwards." She shuddered. "A very nasty piece of work, as Freddie would say."

"Freddie?"

"You haven't forgotten? Your stepfather-in-law to be," she said, laughing. She went on talking about this, about that, about nothing in particular. But when they were drinking their coffee, "I've written Mother about you," she said.

"Well? She disapproves?"

"Of course, she'd disapprove of anyone. She wants to see you. She'd like us to come to Europe on our honeymoon," said Letty carelessly.

"That's out of the question, isn't it?" David asked her. "Even if I'd let you go to Europe with things as they are, even with me to protect you. We'll have to take our honeymoon in snatches, here. But I promise you in a year or two we'll have a real trip," he told her.

"I don't mind," said Letty. "David, you'll come to Rivermead first chance you have?"

He said regretfully, "Try to understand, honey. This is a full-time job. Most weekends I couldn't get away at all. I have to catch up on so much." He smiled at her, begging her comprehension. "The man whose place I took has been on the job for a couple of years. It's a matter of weeks with me."

She said, "Well, there's no harm asking, is there?"

He thought, dismally, If we're sensible we'll postpone the wedding. Until Mac gets back. Until I'm free.

She said, "I thought, the middle of October? Just you and me with Simpie and

Uncle Dick for witnesses?"

Sugar and spice. So infinitely desirable, so astonishingly pretty. She added:

"There's Hot Springs, it's nice then. Or Sea Island. Or we could go to Miami and fly somewhere. Jamaica? How do you get to Nassau? I've never been to Nassau. You can fly to Puerto Rico too, David."

He said gently:

"Darling, I couldn't take the time. Not now. Perhaps after the job's done, and before I go back to the Talbot office —"

"Okay, we'll take a bus ride and go to the movies." She smiled at him. "I'm going to have my hands full with you, Mr. Alcott. Do you always get your way?"

When they left the little restaurant he called a taxi and took her to her hotel. Simpson wasn't in town with her and the apartment was closed. In the taxi she leaned back against his arm with her eyes shut. She said, "Let's not talk. David, will you telephone me, every day? I'll be in town for good in two weeks. You'll have time for me, won't you, just a little?"

She was sweet, she was reasonable . . . she understood. He walked all the way home, a young man with bells in his heart, wings on his heels, despite the smothering blanket of humidity.

CHAPTER 12

The minor fish, mere sardines to be fed to Con, had talked. They didn't know much but what they knew they uttered. So after that David spent much time down on the water fronts, talking over coffee in little dumps, over stew in Greasy Spoons, to his friends the dock workers and taxi drivers. He made more visits to Welfare Island. And he felt he was getting somewhere.

Then one of the taxi drivers was found in the river just as Anderson had been, and things began to happen.

It was the first week in October. Letty was back in town. She was buying her trousseau. She and Simpson had had a terrific battle. Simpie had said firmly, "Of course, Letty, when you marry I'll do what I've wanted to do for years, I'll retire." Simpie had enjoyed a good salary and had saved most of it.

Letty wouldn't hear of that. She said, "Nonsense, Simpie, a vacation if you insist, but who'll look after me and David, who'll run the flat and Rivermead and who'll bring up my mother's grandchildren?"

After the smoke had cleared away, it was observed that Simpie flew a flag of surrender. She would stay on. As a matter of fact, she had been terrified for fear Letty wouldn't want her to stay.

In the brief times they had together David and Letty had decided that, after all, his Village flat was a little too small to accommodate her and her trunks, to say nothing of Simpie. So they'd live in her apartment for the time being. It was big enough . . . room there even for Con, said Letty, grown fond of the black cat, no longer lean, no longer a scrawny kitten but developing rapidly into sleek attractive adolescence.

They were to be married, quietly, on October fifteenth. On the tenth David came home to the Village flat, very late. His things were all packed. The Morriseys would inherit most of his furniture.

When he let himself in he found a light burning, as it had burned the night Letty had allured the janitor. But Letty wasn't there. Con wasn't there either, Con who usually came purring around David's feet, who greeted him always with sound and fury of welcome, and loud catcalls.

David walked up to his desk. Con was there, after all, lying across the desk. He had been strangled. There was a note on the desk. It said, when David could see sufficiently to read it, that the writer didn't like cats, or David . . .

David sat down with the limp small body across his knee. The blood burned back of his eyes, and the tears. Con had loved and trusted him. Con would have been better off leading his hunted life, half starved in alleys, than living on sardines and raw meat, on milk and salmon, with David.

It was a ground-floor flat, rear. A little parched garden went with it. David had no spade, but he managed to scratch a place for Con with his hands and to put him there in a small box and to cover him again. Then he went back, washed his hands, took up the note carefully, folded it in paper and put it in his pocket. Not that he expected fingerprints. There hadn't been any on the package which Morrisey had been handed at the gangplank.

He went out and called a taxi . . .

Letty came running to the door, hearing his voice in the hall. She wore pajamas and her hair was tied up on top of her head. She cried:

"Darling! But you didn't telephone."

"No," he said.

She looked at him quickly.

"What's happened?"

He stalked ahead of her into the big living room and looked around as if he had never seen it before, its gracious charm, its spaciousness, its unobtrusive luxury.

"Sit down," said Letty. "Cigarette? Shall I get you a drink?"

"No; where's Simpie?"

"At the movies. I was trying on clothes. David, what's happened?"

He said dully:

"Letty, we can't be married on the fifteenth."

She began to laugh. "Can't be —" She broke off and took his hands. "But you're serious," she said in a small voice, "you mean it. But, why, David, *why?*"

He said, after a moment:

"I was crazy to think . . . Look, darling, after I'm through with the D.A.'s office. Then — but not now."

"You'll have to explain a little more fully, I think," she said.

He couldn't. He couldn't say, I'm in danger, and if you're my wife you'll be in danger too. You're in danger this minute, if anyone knows about you. He said wearily:

"I can't. Try and understand, trust me if

226

you can. This case I'm on now. It will take all my time. I — I won't be able to be with you, Letty, I'll have to be away so much . . . I'll write, of course . . ." He broke off and looked at her miserably. "All I can say is that when I'm free —"

She said, "You've been begging me, for months!"

"I know."

"And now I'm to sit back and fold my hands and wait. Well, I won't," said Letty roundly, "and that's that. Either the fifteenth, David Alcott, or not at all!"

He said, "I'm sorry . . . I'm sorrier than I can say. I shouldn't — I had no right."

She said, "That doesn't make sense. What do you mean you had no right?" She thought, He's met someone else. She looked at him, at the utter misery and determination stamped on his tired young face and she knew that he hadn't met anyone else and never would. But she hardened her heart. She said, "Well, make up your mind!"

"Then," said David slowly, "it's — not at all."

He got to his feet and went heavily toward the door. He heard her say in a tight, high voice, "It's a good thing we haven't told anyone but Simpie and Uncle Dick."

The door closed. Letty stood there, motionless. She felt as if she had been beaten. She kept thinking, *It's a good thing* . . .

She went back into the living room and sat down to wait for Simpie.

David went out and called a taxi. Richard Talbot was in town. He had not seen him much lately. He drove to the big, old-fashioned apartment and was ushered into the library. Talbot rose from his desk to greet him. He said heartily, "This is a surprise — I —" and then sharply, "What's wrong, David?"

David sat down. His knees shook. Talbot shoved a bottle toward him and a glass. He suggested, "When you've had a drink —"

David had the drink and then he set down the glass. He said, "I've just seen Letty. I told her we couldn't be married until this job is over. I couldn't tell her why."

"Why?" asked Talbot.

David told him about Con. He said, "I can't expose her to this, Mr. Talbot. After the job's over, when I'm back with you, well, they may not be too interested in me then. But I can't risk it now."

"Why didn't you tell her that?"

"You don't know Letty," said David, trying to smile, "she would have married me

228

if she'd had to gag and chloroform me. Besides, I'd rather she didn't know. She'll see you, of course. And you mustn't tell her."

"All right," said Talbot, frowning. "I won't. I'm sorry, David."

That was all he had to tell Letty when she came storming into his office the next day. That he was sorry, that David undoubtedly had good reasons, connected with his work, that if she loved the boy she'd wait, she'd trust him. Simpie had said that too. But Letty wouldn't listen. Why should she trust him, she demanded, when he wouldn't trust her? It was all over, she hoped never to see him again. Never. And she was going south, next week.

October was blue and gold, as it had been last year. November was cold and rainy. There were pictures of Miss Letty McDonald in the papers. Miss McDonald at Hot Springs . . .

More quiet raids, more small fish, days on the docks, in New York, in Brooklyn. A trip to the Canadian border, a plane trip out west to interview a man who had been picked up there. So many of the threads led back to the tall dark gentleman who had come down a gangplank and handed a package to Morrisey. He wasn't the rose, so to speak, but he was at least the thorn. He wasn't the brains of the ring, there were too many brains. But he was a bigger fish than the little catches had brought in thus far. But you couldn't find him, anywhere.

Con had no successor. David missed him, and kept on missing him. He had been real and friendly, without evasion. He ate when he hungered, he slept when he was drowsy, he sat on your lap when he wished his ears rubbed and his white waistcoat tickled. He was glad to see you when you came. He lived much of the time in a strange, indifferent, regal world but he loved you, he was a companion.

David's human companions were men, slow-spoken, with hard jaws and cautious eyes or quick and nervous with tremendous energy. He and Ryan were friends; Adams too, the other special detective. David knew all about them. Ryan with a wife and two kids, and Adams the perennial bachelor, always just missing the matrimonial noose. He knew them inside and out. And they liked him. He came to the office eager to learn, putting on no airs, wearing no topper. A sound youngster who could work twenty-four hours a day if necessary and never ask for quarter. Everyone in the D.A.'s office liked him. And Mac had liked him too. The D.A. flew out twice to see Mac, who was in Arizona now and getting better rapidly.

Twice before the first of the year David's apartment was ransacked. The second time the landlord asked him to move. Such things were hushed up, but they made the landlord nervous. David understood. He put his things in storage and went to live in the house where Adams had rooms. It was an obscure place and obscurity was just as well at this stage.

Down on the docks, a bright early winter day, loafing, in old clothes, a battered hat pulled down over his eyes, watching a little freighter slide in and unload. Romantic, hell . . . routine! And much of the routine was paper work. And much more of it hammering patiently on the unstable anvil of wits dulled by drugs. Sometimes David crawled with repulsion and pity, listening to these abject, degraded creatures, forcing himself to hammer at them again and again.

Pat Morrisey helped him. Pat knew, after all, something of the events leading up to the tragedy which had befallen his sister. He wouldn't tell, on the stand. He had to save her face, poor girl. He couldn't speak of her then. But he could now, to David. And that slow, long search went on and this time another fish came into the net, a little bigger, a little more defiant.

But that day on the docks. Nothing happened, but someone saw him. Later he was followed, he and Ryan. Nothing happened either. They thought they had been mistaken. But that night, walking home alone to the rooming house, the gun cracked and the shot went singing by, too close for laughter. The street spouted people like mushrooms, talking, exclaiming. The cop on the beat came running. No trace of the man, no trace of anything. David had a talk with the cop, he had a talk with the sergeant. There was no word of all that in the papers. But after that David, like Mac, began to walk alone. He didn't want anyone with him, if he could help it, not even Ryan or Adams.

A week later he had someone with him, a witness. He'd dug him up in a pretty bad place. He kept him with him, in his room, on a cot. He needed him, he took no chances. When the day came for his bigger fish to be tried, he wanted that witness whole and intact. And so he took him in and kept him.

He wasn't a very entertaining companion, but you couldn't help that. This sort of job meant strange bedfellows.

He didn't think of Letty consciously. He had too much on his mind. He had to think of what he was doing, to be alert, to keep his wits about him. Unconsciously she was there all the time . . . an undercurrent, sweet and heady . . . a remembrance of things past. And at night, when he slept, he dreamed of her. The three days he had his witness under lock and key he didn't sleep. Daytimes Ryan sat in the room with the witness, or Adams, and food was sent in from the nearest restaurant. At night David lay awake, and listened. And Adams was next door.

Three days and then the trial and the witness who hadn't gone the way of a lot of other witnesses, and the slightly bigger fish behind the bars where, for a very long time, he could do no harm.

This fish was Mopey, for whom they had angled for a long time. A feather in the office cap. The papers were articulate on the subject. What the paper didn't know was how small a cog in the machine Mopey really was. Or that, resentful and malicious, he had done considerable talking, once his sentence was pronounced.

Now the trail led to Harlem and meantime a young man who sold cigarettes in bulk, and candy, on a high school corner, was no longer at his usual stand. There was the evidence under your nose, and the implications sickened you. Witnesses weren't easy to procure, boys and girls, whose parents weren't quite that public-spirited, whose parents wanted things hushed up. But at last there was a lad who came forward and said, "Yes, I bought the cigarettes."

You paid a couple of cents apiece, and in the lot there'd be one, different from the others. And maybe you'd be curious enough to go back the second time and see if you couldn't get another.

Harlem, by night. This was Mopey's doing. David went into various places and took a table and watched the dancing and listened to the music. No one noticed him. Another jitterbug, another gone crazy on jam. He'd learned a good deal about swing, talking to its exponents, reading, trying to train his ears. That was why he went places in Harlem, to listen to jam sessions. He learned to shout at the right time. Another crazy white boy, swing whacky . . .

Sometimes Adams came, or Ryan, or

both, but they didn't sit with him.

They were there at different tables the night that Letty came in after the theater, after the Stork Club, with Bibi Parker, Bibi's new heart, and others. David's table was crowded, with youngsters he'd encountered here and at other places, musicians out of work, mostly. He was buying them drinks. Ryan and Adams were quiet, over in a corner.

Bibi's party was noisy. They'd never been here before. They thought it was marvelous.

Bibi screamed under cover of the music and clutched Letty's arm. She cried, "Isn't that your long-lost? He carries the torch in funny places, doesn't he?"

Letty looked up and saw David and he turned, hearing Bibi's voice and saw her. His heart was crazier than the drums. But he looked right through her. He didn't know her, he had never seen her before.

"Well, for Pete's sake!" said Bibi, agog.

Letty said airily:

"We never speak when we pass by. Skip it, darling."

Bibi said, "Shall we go? There are other places." She was all bright curls and interest. She tried again. "Let's go, if you'd rather." It would make such a wonderful story. Letty couldn't take it. The old heart-beat had cut her dead and Letty couldn't take it.

"We'll stay," said Letty.

David wrote something on a menu and beckoned a waiter. The waiter came, and departed. Adams read the note, rose quietly, and went to a phone booth outside. He called Pat Morrisey's number. He spoke to Pat. Presently he returned to his table.

Pat's flat wasn't too far from Harlem. He could get there in fifteen minutes in a taxi. He got there and did as he was told, sitting at the corner table, half in the darkness, with Ryan and Adams.

The trail had led here. David had not known that it would lead to Bibi's slumming party. He thought, not watching them, that the man had been a fool to suggest this place. Perhaps he hadn't.

Night after night David had been here, waiting. Twice he had just missed his man, but the second time he had seen him. He was seeing him again tonight, at Bibi's table, very attentive to Bibi, a tall dark man, well-dressed, and not young, with good features and a little close-clipped mustache.

He looked over at Ryan's table and Pat nodded, slightly.

This wasn't the time to make your arrest, not with Letty there and Bibi and the other girls and the pleasant, slightly silly young men whom David had never seen before. But you had to make it now, or perhaps never.

David overturned his glass. Ryan and Adams rose, without haste. And Pat, having had his orders, sat where he was, drawing back farther into the darkness. The drums beat and the saxes howled and a lithe black boy was going to town with a cornet . . .

David walked over to Bibi's table and put his hand on the Brazilian's shoulder. He did not look at Letty nor at Bibi, exclamatory and astonished. He said:

"I wonder if you would excuse yourself for a moment."

Adams was doing what he knew was necessary, he didn't have to be told. He was saying quietly to the gaping young men, "Get going, and take the girls with you." He was herding them from the table, with the voice of authority and a badge. And the Brazilian was expostulating. He was talking about his consulate and his government . . . one wondered which consulate and which government. He hadn't been a Brazilian before.

Adams had his particular situation in

hand and Ryan was just behind David . . . Adams was shooing Bibi and her party as if they were chickens. The music kept on playing, the people at near-by tables were watching. They weren't interfering, most of them knew better.

The girls were on their feet now and the two boys, who knew authority when they saw it. They were moving away from the table. Letty looked back. He hadn't looked at her, he hadn't looked at her.

David's hand was still on the Brazilian's arm . . . it was a firm hand. He was saying, "And now, if you please . . ."

"No you don't," said Ryan suddenly, as the knife ripped up and out. Ryan had that arm now, twisting it. The knife tinkled to the floor. It was all very quick and almost noiseless. David's wrist was bleeding. But Ryan's gun was apparent and the Brazilian shrugged his shoulders.

Going down to Headquarters in the taxi, with Ryan and Adams, Pat and the Brazilian, David asked suddenly:

"What happened to — the others?"

"Taxi. I did some explaining. They went — quiet," said Adams, grinning. "I was always a fool for blondes."

Ryan said, "We ought to stop at a doctor's."

"It's just a scratch," said David. The Brazilian said nothing, eloquently. He had recognized Pat. He wouldn't walk down gangplanks anymore. He thought, if I pay for this I won't be the only one.

He was not the game fish, but he was the biggest one to come to the net as yet. He was no more a Brazilian than Pat was. He was an American, born of a Cuban father and a Chilean mother. He had a lot of explaining to do. He had lived for many years in South America and his papers were in order. He'd have to explain that, and his various passports.

He was a good loser. He grinned when Pat said, "You hadn't ought to have grown that mustache again, mister."

It was late when David got back to the rooming house. His wrist had been attended to and the district attorney had been roused from sleep to listen to a report of this early morning's doings. And now David went upstairs to his room and there was Letty.

He said, "You turn up in the damnedest places. How'd you get here?"

"Adams. He's a darling."

"He's a fool. I'll kill him when he comes back. He stopped for coffee."

"Don't. I just told him that — that —"

"That what?"

He stood there staring at her. He was dead tired and his wrist hurt. All he wanted to do was sleep. He said, "You should stay away from Harlem. More than anything, you should stay away from me."

She said irrelevantly, "I like your landlady. I've been down in her parlor. She got up and made me some tea. She's swell. I told her —"

"What did you tell her and Adams?"

"That I loved you," said Letty, "and we'd had a fight and I couldn't bear it another minute."

"You're crazy —" he said gloomily — "you and Adams *and* the landlady!"

The room was impersonal, it wasn't much of a room. Letty looked around it. She asked:

"You've been living here?"

"I have."

"Where's Con?"

"He's dead," said David, with his jaw set.

She gave a little cry. "I — I liked Con." She came closer to David. She said humbly:

"Wouldn't you kiss me?"

He put his arm around her, the wrong arm. He flinched, and she said, "What's the matter?" Then she saw the bandage.

She said, after a moment, "Adams didn't tell me that."

"He had no business telling you anything. It's nothing. Bibi's Brazilian had a knife."

"Adams just said," said Letty, "that he was someone you'd been looking for. I don't understand, I won't try to, I won't ask questions. Is that why you wouldn't marry me, David, in October?"

He said, "That's why."

Letty was very white. Her teeth began to chatter. She said, shaking:

"I'm scared, David, I'm scared stiff. How long will this last?"

"Till Mac's back."

She said:

"I won't pester you, I won't try to see you, I won't come here again."

"You're darn tootin' you won't," he said, "I'll probably move tomorrow."

She said, "Look, David, if I don't get in your way, if I wait, then when Mac comes back — ?"

He said slowly, "Perhaps I have no right —"

Letty stamped her foot. She cried, "Make up your mind!"

He was very tired. Adams would be along in a minute. Adams would have to take Letty home, it would be safer. David was too tired to move, anyway. He didn't have to move. She was in his arms. She was crying, she was laughing. She was saying:

"You spend all your time putting people in jail, first me, now Bibi's Brazilian. But I'll never be free, David, don't you know that? Never!"

He heard Adams's heavy step on the stairs. In a moment he'd knock at the door. His arms closed about Letty and he didn't feel the pain this time. He knew that she was right. They belonged together. They'd fight their way through life and they'd love it. He kissed her, hard and long. There was Adams at the door. David smacked Letty gently where she should have been smacked harder, earlier in her youth. He said, "I love you, Letty, and I'll be seeing you, when Mac comes back."

Adams knocked.

"Come in," said David, "I've a job for you. A brunette job, this time."

Adams came in, sheepish. A flat-footed Cupid. He said, "So she found you, Dave."

"She found me," said David, "and she's going to lose me again. Take her away, get her out of here, if you have to lock her up."

Letty was powdering her nose. She

grinned at Adams. She looked at David. It was morning, it was sunrise, it was all the future. She said cheerfully:

" 'Bye, darling. Take care of yourself." Her smile faded but she clung to it with determination. "Be seein' you," she told him, "when Mac gets back. It's a date."

"It's a date," agreed David.

The door closed on them and he stumbled happily to bed.

We hope you have enjoyed this Large Print book. Other Thorndike Press or Chivers Press Large Print books are available at your library or directly from the publishers.

For more information about current and upcoming titles, please call or write, without obligation, to:

Publisher
Thorndike Press
295 Kennedy Memorial Drive
Waterville, ME   04901
Tel. (800) 223-1244
Tel. (800) 223-6121

OR

Chivers Press Limited
Windsor Bridge Road
Bath BA2 3AX
England
Tel. (0225) 335336

All our Large Print titles are designed for easy reading, and all our books are made to last.